Sisters, Sup~~~~~~, Slushy, Gushy Love Songs

"Chazza says Q's a total creep! This guy's really, really full of himself, *really* arrogant – the rest of the lads in the band can't stand him!"

"So," I frowned, as Tor giggled and wriggled his way out of Rowan's grasp, "what are they all doing being in a band with him, if they don't like him?"

"It's Q's band," Rowan explained. "He started it up."

"Q's a stupid name," Tor announced breathlessly, now that he'd escaped from Rowan's tickling clutches.

"Yeah – and Q might just be a stupid boy," Rowan muttered, shooting me a worried glance.

Linn could be a grouch sometimes, but she was *our* grouch.

What was she getting herself into? And did we dare ask her?*

(*Are you *kidding*?)

Find out more about Ally's World at
www.karenmccombie.com

ALLY'S WORLD

SiSTERS, SUPER-CREEPS and SLUSHY, GUSHY LOVE SONGS

KAREN McCOMBIE

SCHOLASTIC

foR cecy (aged 14), eveN though she's NeveR Read ANY
of MY books. (she keePs MaKiNg excuses about how haRd
it is to.tuRN tHe Pages wheN You'Ve ONLY got PaWs.)

Scholastic Children's Books,
Commonwealth House, 1–19 New Oxford Street,
London WC1A 1NU, UK
A division of Scholastic Ltd
London ~ New York ~ Toronto ~ Sydney ~ Auckland
Mexico City ~ New Delhi ~ Hong Kong

First published in the UK by Scholastic Ltd, 2002

Copyright © Karen McCombie, 2002
Cover illustration copyright © Spike Gerrell, 2002

ISBN 0 439 99357 1

Typeset by TW Typesetting, Midsomer Norton, Somerset
Printed and bound in Great Britain by Cox & Wyman Ltd, Reading, Berkshire.

10 9 8 7 6 5 4 3 2 1

Contents

PROLOGUE

Dear Mum,

You know something funny? I always thought that you and Dad were each other's first loves.

I don't know *why* I supposed that; probably just because it seems more romantic to think that way. Plus, there's the fact that it's a bit ... well, *blee* to imagine your parents snogging someone else – like you might have had another mum or dad, if things had turned out differently.

Urgh – *way* too weird to think about...

Anyway, the other night, Rowan mentioned that her mate Chazza's band had been offered the chance to play at the Electric Ballroom in Camden (as a support band to the support band – so don't get *too* impressed), and Dad came out with, "Oh, I used to go to the Electric Ballroom all the time with Marianne!"

Well, you could have heard a doll-size pin drop in the living room as me, Linn, Rowan and Tor just turned and stared at him. So Dad ends up explaining to us all that this Marianne was your predecessor; some girl whose hobbies seemed to be dancing, wearing red lipstick and sulking, by the sounds of it. Still, sulky or not, at least Dad's first love had a reasonable name. I couldn't believe yours was someone called *Spud*.

Honestly, Mum – how could you have dated a *Spud*? And how did he get that name? Did he *look* like a potato, or something? I asked Grandma, but she says she can't remember him. I think what she means is that she doesn't *want* to remember him. And I think that's what's going to happen with Grandma and Q...

Yep, you read that right: Q. And that *is* a name, by the way (or so he told us). Q is the name of Linn's first love. Does that sound strange, knowing that your Love Child No. 1 fell for someone? It was definitely strange for me and Rowan, mainly because we couldn't *stand* the guy.

OK, I'd better start my story of Linn (and her ever changing moods), Q (and his ever expanding big head), and me (and my attempts to become the new Noel Gallagher – only prettier, hopefully).

Love you lots,

Ally

(your Love Child No. 3)

PS Did you ever say, "I love you, Spud"? And did you manage to do it without laughing?

Chapter 1

TUNE IN TO ALLY'S WORLD FM...

"Is that the sound of a cat being strangled?"

The record I'd just stuck on was getting very different reactions from my two friends. Sandie was swaying in time to the dreamy high vocals and happily humming along out of tune, while Salma was doing what can only be described as *gurning*.

"*No*," I said to Salma. "That is *not* the sound of a cat being strangled. That's Kate Bush."

"Who?" Salma frowned.

"Kate Bush," I repeated. "She was big in the seventies. Or maybe it was the eighties. Anyway, that's her on the album cover. Doesn't she look amazing?"

"Hmm. So, what are you listening to old rubbish like this for?" asked Salma, flipping the LP cover back and forth and studying it as if it was a highly toxic alien life form. Salma's taste in music is whatever's in the Top Ten that particular week. Give her any record more than a month old and she thinks it's as out of touch as crinolines and handlebar moustaches.

"Actually, I'm working my way through my mum's record collection," I explained. "Kate Bush was – *is* – one of her favourites."

That shut her up. Salma, along with all my friends, would never take the mickey out of anything to do with Mum.

Mind you, it was hard to concentrate on Kate Bush, *or* on the conversation I was having with Salma and Sandie, when I could hear – from somewhere else in the house – the sound of what *might* be a cat getting strangled. I hoped my brother Tor was taking his babysitting duties seriously, and was watching over Salma's rampant posse of small relatives.

Salma had interrupted mine and Sandie's lazy Saturday afternoon listening to Mum's old records only five minutes before. She'd turned up on my doorstep on a mission of mercy, looking frazzled, and accompanied by three grinning, dark-haired toddlers all holding hands but also all bound to her by individual, dayglo-coloured kid-leashes that linked their wrists to Salma's. After spending the afternoon in Priory Park trying to tire out the twins (her kid sisters, Rosa and Julia) and her niece (Laurel), Salma had rounded them up and was shooing them home for their tea, when all three announced in unison that they needed to go to the loo. Coincidentally, they were passing our house.

Actually, it wasn't all *that* coincidental; they often seem to need the loo *just* in sight of our house. I think it's the lure of countless pets to gawp at and chase, plus they all seem to have three-year-old crushes on older-man Tor (a mature seven) – there's always one or another of them trying to smother him in cuddles in-between traumatizing the animals by petting them so hard they practically *fracture* something, or eating the food right out of their bowls. (By the way, I never knew rabbits could growl until the time I found Rosa in the rabbit run eating the sliced carrots and soggy lettuce meant for Cilla the bunny. As Rosa munched, Cilla had a look on her face that reminded me of Arnold Schwarzenegger in those old *Terminator* movies. I'm not kidding. If that rabbit had access to an Uzi machine gun right at that moment, I wouldn't have fancied Rosa's chances much.)

That's the trouble with Salma's small relations: they're VERY everything, never *slightly* something. What I mean is, they're VERY loud, VERY enthusiastic and VERY fast. Which makes Tor VERY confused; he never knows which mini-tornado to watch out for next, they spin around him so fast. Still, when you're the youngest kid in the family, it's your job to entertain tiny visiting children. That's just the law, isn't it?

"Do you want a Coke or something?" I asked Salma, getting up and grabbing mine and Sandie's empty glasses off the coffee table.

"Wouldn't mind some orange juice, if you've got any," Salma muttered in her husky voice, tilting her head to one side so that her long, thick, shiny dark hair tumbled over one shoulder. She was studying our vast collection of ancient LPs (the living room is a CD-free zone), but I knew she wouldn't have a clue who any of the bands or singers were, apart from maybe the Beatles and the Rolling Stones. Between my mum's hippy-dippy rock-chick collection and Dad's weird assortment (fifties rock'n'roll, reggae, some punk and even – eek! – a few second-hand country albums he's bought since he started *line*-dancing), there was nothing she'd recognize from MTV.

"Back in a sec," I called out as I stepped out of the living room and away from the wailing wonderfulness of Kate Bush's voice and into the chaos of the hall.

One of Salma's brood (I can never tell them apart) was careering head-first on her tummy down the stairs, screaming with excitement while cats scattered to the wind and more small girls and Rolf and Winslet yelled and barked encouragement from the the first-floor landing.

"All right, Ally Pally?" Dad smiled at me, looking up from the bike he was clattering to bits on the hall floor. After a day's hard work dismantling bikes round at the shop, you wouldn't think he'd be in the mood to do the same at home, but playing with spanners and getting covered in oil seems to be one of his hobbies.

"Wouldn't you be better off doing that in the kitchen?" I suggested to Dad, above the sound of the tinny radio blasting by his side and the shrill screeches of "ME next! ME next!" coming from the top of the staircase.

"Can't – it's already been taken," Dad grinned. "Bit of a belly-dancing workshop going on through there..."

I took a couple of steps along the hall, peered into the kitchen and saw what he meant. It looked (and sounded) like a Moroccan bazaar in there, with swathes of material draped over the table, the chairs, the sink and even the clothes-horse as Rowan whirred like a demon on her rickety old sewing machine, making up some exotic costume or other. Her mate Von, meanwhile, had yet more

Indian-type fabric draped around her, and was hip-thrusting her way past the washing machine in time to yodelling Arabic music.

"I wouldn't have recognized it as the kitchen if you hadn't told me," I grinned at Dad, as I walked back towards him. "Anyway, do you want a – *oof!* – cup of tea or something?"

A Rosa/Julia/Laurel had just slithered down the stairs at high speed and cracked my ankle bone with her head. From the way she bounced up giggling, it seemed her skull was made out of invincible titanium or whatever space rockets are made out of, guaranteed to withstand the force of intense heat, intense cold, random meteor showers and the fragile bones of lesser mortals like myself.

"Aaargh! *Nooooo!*" I heard Tor yelp from somewhere upstairs as he saw that the next Rosa/Julia/Laurel was all set to project herself down the stairs while clutching Mad Max the hamster, whom she must have smuggled out of his cage when Tor wasn't looking.

"Give the hamster to Tor!" I shouted urgently up the stairs.

"But he wants to *play!*" squealed the Rosa/Julia/Laurel who'd thundered into me and was now thundering her way back up to the first-floor landing.

"Let *go*!" Tor yelped again, trying to rescue Mad Max from Rosa/Julia/Laurel's grasp.

But Mad Max was perfectly able to rescue himself. Sensing that being squeezed by tiny fingers and sent hurtling down the staircase were two things he was *not* keen on, Mad Max did what came naturally (for him, being a psycho in fur) and bit Rosa/Julia/Laurel.

Hard.

It was at this point that Linn walked in through the front door – home from her Saturday job – and proceeded to trip over a disembodied bike wheel, skid along the hall floor, and come to rest flat-out by the foot of the bannister, narrowly missing the slalom run the *third* Rosa/Julia/Laurel had done while the other two were arguing, being bitten or screaming.

For just the merest microsecond, I was *so* stunned I couldn't say anything – same went for Dad. But as Linn pushed herself up, with her hair tumbling out of its tight ponytail and oil smeared on her neatly pressed white shirt, all the rest of the noise in the house seemed suddenly amplified: Sandie and Salma yelling at each other above the sound of Kate Bush trilling; Dad's radio shrilling away while dogs barked, little girls shrieked and Tor roared; the Middle Eastern disco blasting out from the kitchen, along with the insistent, rattling hammer of our Stone Age sewing machine.

"Are you … are you OK?" I asked Linn, snapping into action and trying to help her up.

In irritation or embarrassment or both, she wrenched her elbow away from me and got to her feet alone.

"I'm *fine*!" Linn growled, un-finely. "God, sometimes I *hate* this house!"

I knew what she meant by that last snarled statement. Linn occasionally has these "I-was-born-into-the-wrong-family!" moments, where she's sure there's a designer-dressed set of parents out there somewhere living in a calm, clutter-free, beautifully kept luxury apartment, wondering whatever happened to their long-lost matching daughter. While here she was, stuck with the Loves in a crumbling, noisy, messy, cat-, kid- and dog-filled madhouse.

And today, right now, she was *definitely* having one of those moments…

"Have you hurt anything, Linnhe?" Dad asked, all concerned.

Oops.

Calling Linn "Linnhe" is a bad move at the best of times. Calling Linn "Linnhe" when she was as mad as this was downright *dangerous*.

"I..." she muttered darkly, as if she was trying to hold back her temper, "am ... going to have a *long* bath."

And with a defiant smoothing back of her hair (which she didn't really want to do, since it just made the smear of oil on her forehead streak right across her blondish hair), Linn stomped up the stairs, sending small girls scurrying out of the way.

"Oh dear!" Dad pulled a face at me, as we heard the bathroom door slam shut.

Then suddenly a high-pitched, metallic whine filled the house, accompanied by seismic judders, as our elderly, cantankerous plumbing system cranked into life.

"*Aaaaarrgghhh! I hate* this house!" came a muffled roar of frustration from inside the bathroom.

"Oh dear..." I nodded back at Dad.

Looked like we were set for a fun weekend tiptoeing around the rumbling volcano that was Linnhe. Sorry – *Linn*.

"Hey, Sandie," I said, rejoining my friends in the living room, "any chance of me moving in with you for a couple of days...?"

Chapter 2

HOW *NOT* TO APPLY LIPSTICK

I'd only been joking when I asked Sandie if I could stay at hers for the weekend. But it seemed like a fantastically good idea once Linn announced that she wanted to kill me.

Why did she want to kill me? Well, I'll give you three (small) reasons...

I think Rosa, Julia and Laurel should get an entry into *The Guinness Book of World Records* for "Wreaking the Most Havoc in the Shortest Space of Time". (Is there a category called that? If there isn't, there should be.) Basically, in the few minutes they'd been in our house, they'd terrorized Tor and liberated the hamsters from their cages in his room, dented my ankle, nearly squashed the life out of Mad Max, covered every surface in the house (including doggy surfaces) with sticky fingerprints, sprayed a can of hair mousse down the toilet and trashed Linn's room.

If they'd trashed any other room in the house, it wouldn't have been so bad, since every one of them (including my own) is so full of clutter and stuff that a bit of mess can go undetected for quite some time. (On a particularly bad clutter day, a flock of Amazonian parakeets could roost in our living room and we probably wouldn't notice.) But in Linn's immaculate, museum-pristine bedroom, the merest ruffle on her white duvet cover, or a bottle of nail varnish not replaced *precisely* in the perfectly symmetrical line of nail varnishes on her dressing table, and my big sister will kick up such a mighty fuss that you'd expect to hear a report about it on *News at Ten*.

So when Linn stomped upstairs to her room while her bath gurgled into life, and then stomped back downstairs screaming, I knew something bad must have happened. What I didn't realize was that the bad thing was all my fault – well, at least that was how *Linn* saw it.

She may have been ranting full-force in my face, but Linn was yelling so fast that I could only make out snatches of what she was saying, which is probably just as well.

"Blah, blah, blah ... complete *state*! Blah, blah, blah ... *ruined*! Blah, blah, blah ... *your* friends! Blah, blah, blah ... could *kill* you!"

(Actually, what I took in wasn't so much "Blah, blah, blah" as a maximum-volume "AAARRRGGHH … complete *state*! AAARRRGGGHH … *ruined*! AAAARRRRGGGGHHH … *your* friends! AAAARRRRGGGGHHH … could *kill* you!")

"Now, now. I'm sure it's not that bad, Linn," Dad stepped in and tried to placate her. "I'm sure we can get it sorted out."

As Dad spoke, Tor scuttled off to the sanctuary of the harem in the kitchen, while Salma made her own bid to get into *The Guinness Book of World Records* by gathering up her terrible tribe by the reins and dragging them out of the house at the speed of light. She was quickly followed by Sandie, who seemed to have decided that staying for tea at our house would be about as much fun as being poked in the eye with a pointy stick.

"Listen, go and relax in your smelly bath, Linn, and Ally Pally will have your room tidied by the time you come out," said Dad, trying to coax Linn out of her fury.

"I don't want Ally anywhere *near* my room, thank you very much!" fumed Linn. "And *please* don't call it a 'smelly bath', Dad – you *know* it's my aromatherapy oils!"

In Linn's parallel universe, she has a discerning, cultured parent who can distinguish between jojoba oil and geranium oil at fifty paces. Sadly, the only oil Linn's real-life parent is familiar with is the type that lubricates bike chains. And expecting Dad to call her regular hour-long aromatherapy soaks anything other than "smelly baths" is about as likely as the chances of him calling me anything other than Ally Pally. And *I* don't take offence, which is *something*, considering I share the same nickname as a large pile of bricks (Alexandra Palace, looming large over Crouch End).

But then, I'm not Linn, who can take offence at thin air if she's in that kind of mood.

"Go on, Ally Pally," Dad nudged me, as soon as we heard the bathroom door slam shut. "Go and see what the damage is in her room and give it a quick tidy up!"

"Huh? But you heard what Linn said!" I protested. Still, one look at Dad's sweet, pleading face sent me scurrying up the stairs.

The thing is, Dad hates the idea of any of us fighting, and we hate the idea of him ever being upset by us. So – despite my very real fear of having my head torn off if I so much as stepped a big toe over the threshold of Linn's room – I decided I'd better do what he thought was best. And if the mess wasn't *too* bad and if I *really* hurried, I could have everything sorted and barricade myself safely in my own attic room across the hall before Linn the She-Devil was out of her smelly bath.

At least that's what I'd thought as I zoomed up the stairs. But when I opened the door to Linn's room, my heart sank two floors down to the bike-strewn hallway. It was *way* worse than I'd expected.

The thing is, Linn's entire room is decorated in various exotic shades of plain white. OK – I exaggerate; maybe there's a couple of cream shades in there, if you want to get pernickety. Her idea of bedroom hell would be to have walls adorned in floral wallpaper, specially if it came with a matching flowery border. And OK, so Salma's three-year-old rellies maybe hadn't sneaked in with a pasting table and several rolls of petally wallpaper, but it wasn't far off. One (or all) of them had come over very artistic, doodling giant, wibbly-wobbly flowers over the bottom half of one white wall, using (Linn's favourite) pink lipstick. The tube of which was now lying used up and empty on the floor.

And I don't know what Rosa/Julia/Laurel had stepped in at the park, but the brownish (hopefully just muddy-ish) footprints they'd trampolined on to the duvet cover were never going to get them into Linn's good books. In fact, it might get them locked in the cupboard next time she saw them.

Right at that second, I realized that I had absolutely no idea how you get lipstick off a painted wall (never mind suspicious brown footprints out of white cotton). I knew Grandma – whose head is like a computer program when it comes to practical stuff – would definitely have some wise-woman remedy up her sleeve, but I didn't have time to phone her, and anyway I was pretty sure she'd said something about going out for the afternoon with her boyfriend Stanley. So I improvised (i.e. I panicked): grabbed a tissue out of the box on Linn's bedside table, spat on it and rubbed at the nearest flower. Which immediately smeared out into a twice-the-original-size, psychedelically fuzzy flower.

Hmm.

It was time to improvise (i.e. panic) some more, so I grabbed a bottle of nail-varnish remover and tried daubing that on with the tissue. It worked about as well as spit – that is, not at all.

OK – now I was *seriously* going to die. Of a heart attack, probably, before Linn got a chance to kill me with her bare hands. I needed to stop panicking and think for a second. I got up from my crouching kneel, plonked myself down on Linn's (white) padded window-seat and stared off out through the panes of glass, as if the sight of the far-off high-rises of central London would offer up some clue as to what I should do next.

Fat chance.

Still, staring out of the window did slightly take my mind off the lipstick disaster. Being banned from this room at all times – like the rest of the family, both two-legged and four-legged – I don't get to admire this view too often. (Except when I launch the occasional secret SAS-style raid to go in and borrow something, of course. And replace it very, *very* carefully, of *course*.)

Dad's bedroom is directly below Linn's, but that couple of metres lower means that all you can see out of his window is the tops of the trees at the bottom of the garden (home to our rescue pigeon, Britney). My room, right across the hall from Linn's, has a pretty groovy view, too, with Ally Pally (me, the flesh-and-blood person) getting to gawp at Ally Pally (the slightly-crumbly-but-amazing brick building).

Actually, our views suit both of us – me and Linn, I mean. I love where we live, and I love seeing the historic palace perched on top of the hill. (Like hippy haven Glastonbury Tor in Somerset, the hill Alexandra Palace sits on is a central crossover point of spooky old ley lines, Mum once told me. Only she left before she could explain exactly what spooky old ley lines *were*.)

And staring out over London suits Linn, since she seems almost desperate to get away from us sometimes, to escape to a different, more organized life somewhere out there. A life where there're no cat hairs on your clothes; a life where you eat posh Marks & Spencer's ready meals instead of watching your kid brother make food collages out of beans and Supernoodles; a life where everyone thinks your name is normal Lynn, not Linnhe, after some remote, plankton-filled loch in Scotland.

Poor Linn – she's nice really, under all that growling she does. I sat there on her window-seat, daydreaming about how much nicer it would be if Linn was nicer more often. But then maybe she needed to be *happier* to be nicer.

"I wish Linn could be happier," I whispered under my breath, as I squeaked the tissue I was still holding over some Rosa/Julia/Laurel-sized fingerprints I'd just spotted on the panes of glass.

Hey, you know how wishes have a habit of coming true, in Disney movies at least? Well, welcome to the *real* world.

"Ally! What are you doing in here? Get OUT of my room NOW!"

"I'm gone!" I yelped, zipping past my lavender-scented black-tempered sister and nearly tripping over Winslet (an empty lipstick case wedged between her canines) as I bolted to the safety of my own room.

Maybe the only way Linn would be happier is if the rest of us troublesome, messy Loves magically vanished – just like *I* wished the lipstick flowers could magically vanish from the wall before Linn saw how much *worse* they'd got, thanks to my crap cleaning efforts.

"ARRRRRGGGGHHHHHH!"

Oops – sounded like she'd spotted that her flowers had bloomed...

Chapter 3

OH, LOOK! IT'S ... ER ... WHASSISNAME

After a busy day's grouching on Saturday, Linn was planning to spend all of Sunday at home, swotting for something or other.

Mmm ... like that was *really* going to improve her mood.

Time for me to find something that would get me safely out of the house (and shouting range) for the afternoon...

"What is she doing?" Billy whispered loudly, nearly blasting my eardrum, he'd leant in so close.

The "she" he was talking about wasn't Linn (she was safely in her room, with her black cloud of gloom for company). And it wasn't Sandie, who was right beside us, or the legions of other girls hovering around outside the MTV building in Camden this Sunday afternoon. The "she" was – of course – Kyra.

Kyra was standing about a metre in front of us, in amongst a crew of girls who were all squealing and jumping so much that you'd think they were standing barefoot in a pit of beetles. Not that Kyra was squealing or jumping. I squinted at her, checked out what exactly she *was* doing, then whispered my reply back to Billy.

"She's posing," I explained.

"Oh," Billy nodded, swivelling his baseball cap the right way around on his head. "*I* thought there was something wrong with her..."

It was an easy mistake to make. Kyra was doing this slouch where one shoulder was tilted down so far that it was in danger of sliding off her body, while the other shoulder was tilted so high it was practically level with her ear. She was also putting all her weight on to just one leg, while trailing the toes of her other foot seductively back and forth along the grubby, chewing-gum splattered pavement. (I'm pretty sure Kyra thought she looked sulky and gorgeous, but really she just looked like a little kid's drawing of a person. You know what I mean: when they scribble their mum all out of proportion, with one leg longer than the other and a nose on the side of her head or something.)

The reason Kyra was pulling the weird shoulder slouch – and the reason Kyra had persuaded me, Sandie and Billy to come down here – was because she'd heard that MTV were expecting a secret appearance by a famous band, who were going to be interviewed for the *Select* show. And the *Select* show just happens to be filmed in a studio that has a huge window out on to the street, so that while the veejays and bands are chatting on the sofa inside, hordes of fans can be seen behind them out on the pavement, screaming, yelling and chucking themselves up against the glass in their attempts to attract the attention of their heroes (and get concussion into the bargain).

Anyway, the "famous" band had finally shown up for their secret appearance. The secret being that my mates and I hadn't a *clue* who they were.

"Have you figured it out yet?" Billy asked, frowning at the so-called celebs in the studio. All we could see from where we were standing were three backs, all of which seemed to belong to somebody male.

"Nope," I shook my head. "I don't recognize them. Have you any idea, Sand?"

Sandie, standing on tiptoes in her wedge sandals, shook her head.

"Kyra must know by now, though," she suggested. "She's so close her breath's practically steaming up the window. Hold on, I'll go and ask her."

"Does this show go out live on MTV, or what?" I asked Billy, as we both watched Sandie wriggle her way through the squealers and jumpers towards Kyra.

"Dunno," Billy shrugged, not very usefully.

"I hope for Kyra's sake that it goes out later," I said. "She'll be really hacked off if she misses seeing herself posing on the telly."

"She's probably set her video," Billy grinned.

That was true. And after all, that *was* the point of this afternoon as far as Kyra was concerned – not just to try and see a famous (ha!) band, but also to try to get her mug on the telly.

Me? I'd just been interested in the idea of noseying at celebs (double ha!) and staying out of Linn's way for the afternoon; I wasn't too bothered about the programme itself, because we didn't have anything as technologically advanced as cable or satellite at home. In fact, we hardly had what normal people would call a TV. Our telly was definitely in need of a visit to the television hospital – it wasn't natural that every colour on the screen was some kind of shade of green. (The other night, it looked like *Top of the Pops* had been recorded on a cross-Channel ferry, everyone seemed so sea-sick green.)

"Kyra doesn't know who it is," said Sandie, coming back over to rejoin us.

"Should have asked those girls beside her," Billy suggested. "They're going *mental* for whoever's inside."

"I *did* ask," Sandie nodded. "They haven't a clue either."

The three of us looked at each other and grinned.

"God, that's it! I want to be in a band!" Billy announced.

"But you can't play anything and you sing like a truck running over a set of bagpipes!" I laughed at him.

"Yeah, but that lot in there might be just as bad," Billy pointed out, "and the girls out here don't seem to care!"

"I see what you mean," I nodded, while shooting my mate a sarky sideways glance. "Maybe you *should* join a band, Billy. After all, it's the only way you'll ever get a girl interested in you."

"Wow, you are *so* funny. *Not*," said Billy, pretending to take offence at my dig. Which of course he didn't really, since it's just our usual way of bugging one another (i.e. communicating).

"But that's not true, Ally! You're forgetting Anita – isn't she, Billy?" Sandie smirked at him. "So how's it going with her – still totally in love?"

Up till this point, Sandie had always been the butt of Billy's wind-ups, but since he'd started seeing Anita – his first ever girlfriend – Sandie had been getting on much better with him. Mainly because, for the first time ever, she'd been able to get her own back on Billy and tease him *rotten*.

Ah, sweet revenge...

"Numumph," mumbled Billy incoherently, turning his head away and pretending to scan the crowd. But even side-on you could see his face – including his *freckles* – blushing bright pink at this sensitive subject.

"Sorry? What did you say" I asked him, holding a hand up to one ear.

Bless. It was cute to see Billy so tongue-tied over a girl. And so much fun to make him suffer over it.

"Numumph!" he muttered, only marginally louder.

"What?" I frowned, trying not to look at Sandie 'cause I knew we'd both burst out giggling.

But he was saved from any more torture over his love life. Something was happening: like starlings flying in synch over the rooftops, or lemmings hurling themselves in droves over cliffs, the crowd around us suddenly began hubbubb-ing and moving away from the plate-glass studio window and towards the gates of the MTV building.

"Kyra!" I yelled, as I spotted her straightening her shoulders and following the herd. "What's going on?"

"The band are coming out in a minute!" she

yelled back excitedly. "I'm going to try and get an autograph!"

"But you don't know who they are!" Billy shouted over at her.

"So?" Kyra frowned, as if he'd uttered just about the dumbest thing anyone had ever bothered uttering.

Billy opened his mouth to say something else, but before he could, he vanished – sent sprawling on the pavement and trampled by a stampede of squealing, jumping girlies, all rushing to meet the amazing … the astounding … the completely … *unknown* pop stars.

Speaking of unknown pop stars, there was one in our living room when I got back home.

I couldn't make out what the noise was when I first arrived, because Rolf set up a barkathon as soon as I walked in through the front door, while Winslet gently but firmly gripped the leg of my jeans between her teeth and dragged me towards the kitchen, in the hope that I might give them both a small advance on their tea.

"What's going on through there?" I asked Dad, recognizing the peaks of his spiky dark hair above the top of the white duvet cover he was struggling to fold.

"It's Chazza," Dad explained, lowering the cover down, then yanking it up quickly so that it didn't trail in the cornflake crumbs that seemed to be littering the kitchen floor. "He's come round to play his band's demo to Rowan and Von."

Oooh – I was intrigued. Rowan had told me before that her mate Chazza had got a band together at college, and right now I really fancied tiptoeing up to the living-room door and listening in properly. But first, I needed to help Dad. He was in serious danger of being swamped by the sea of laundry he'd started to do. Course, the muddle of dirty stuff, washed stuff and dried stuff wasn't helped by the fact that the entire kitchen table was covered by oily bike bits on newspaper (leftovers from yesterday's bicycle dissection), and the fact that Tor was building some kind of cardboard fort thing on the floor out of not quite empty cereal boxes.

"Here – give me a corner of that," I said, stepping over Tor, then Rolf, then Winslet, and making a grab for one end of Linn's newly laundered duvet cover.

At the same time, the music suddenly blasted louder from the living room, as someone (Chazza, probably) cranked up the volume to get the full effect of a screaming guitar solo (Chazza's, presumably).

"What did you say?" Dad squinted at me, talking above the guitar screech and the accompanying dog howls from a perplexed Rolf.

"Give me the corner!" I yelled above the racket, not watching my step and accidentally demolishing half a cornflake-packet turret, which set Tor off whining.

And then came another, scarier noise.

"AAAAAAAAAARRRRRGGGGGGHHHH!"

The roar at the kitchen door wasn't loud enough to be heard in the living room over Chazza's finest (?) moment, but it certainly shut me, Dad, Tor and the dogs up.

"What *IS* it with this place?!" Linn growled, her face as white and clenched as her fists.

"Um…" mumbled Dad, struggling to find some answer that might soothe Linn.

Ha.

"Why is everything so *NOISY*! How am I meant to study in this … this *PIT*!" Linn raged on.

"It's … it's just laundry," Dad said feebly, wafting his hand towards the clothes-horse, as though the kitchen floor and table were visions of polished, uncluttered loveliness and not littered with mechanical gubbins and cornflake crumbs.

"I can't *LIVE* like this any more!" Linn buried her face in her hands.

Dad looked at Linn in a panic, looked at me as though I might have a clue about what to do (wrong), then went over and wrapped his arms around her. Amazingly, she let him, and I was pretty sure I heard the snuffling of tears going on.

"Tor," I whispered, an idea of how to help suddenly coming to me. "Go and ask Rowan to turn the music down, please."

In a flash, Tor scooted off, while Rolf and Winslet helped the situation in their own, crunchy way by starting to hoover up the crumbs from the kitchen floor. Using just their tongues, of course.

"It's OK, Linn," Dad said soothingly, as he stroked her hair.

(*Not too much, Dad*, I found myself thinking. Mussing up Linn's hair was a sure-fire way of winding her up again.)

"Listen – *I* know what'll cheer you up!" he continued, a smile snapping on to his worried face as something occurred to him.

"What?" Linn sniffed, raising her head off his chest and looking expectantly into his face, wondering what the something might be.

I think she was hoping he might say that he'd decided to give the contents of the house away to our local Oxfam shop, paint the entire place magnolia, and sell me, Rowan and Tor to slave traders on cocoa plantations, but no such luck.

"Let's all go out to the movies! Right now! As a family!" Dad beamed at her. "I'm sure there's a teatime showing of that new Disney film at the Odeon. My treat!"

I'll give Linn her due – she covered up her disappointment pretty well. Obviously, the idea of spending *more* time with her family from hell wasn't exactly at the top of her list of Fabulous Things to Do (specially when it involved sitting through a U-rated movie), but she somehow managed to force her mouth into a strained smile for Dad's sake.

Still, one thing was for sure: I was going to do my best to bagsy the cinema seat furthest away from Linn, in her current guise as Queen Grouch…

Chapter 4

BEWARE – FEARSOME GUARD BLOBS...

The movie had been corny but bearable (a cartoon thing about dogs, which went down a storm with Tor, of course). The pizza Dad had treated us to afterwards was very nice (even if Linn's badly hidden bad mood gave me slight indigestion). And the evening was so nice we'd decided to walk home instead of jump on the bus (with me, Ro and Tor zipping ahead and leaving Dad to suffer Linn's charming company alone).

"Um ... till Tuesday. Wednesday at the latest," said Rowan, swinging one of Tor's hands in hers, her multicoloured metal bracelets tinkling together on her wrist.

"Three days?" I raised my eyebrows at her, while I swung Tor's other hand in mine. "That's a bit hopeful, isn't it?"

"What?" Tor asked, now that he'd finished humming the theme tune of the movie we'd just seen and tuned into what me and Ro were saying.

"We're taking bets on how long Linn's grumpy

mood's going to last for," Rowan bent over and hissed in his ear, casting a quick glance over her shoulder to check that Dad and Linn were still walking far enough behind us not to overhear.

"Oh," Tor nodded, looking thoughtful, although it was hard to work out what exactly those thoughts might be. But, hey, that's normal with Tor.

"And I could have done without her sarky comments about Chazza's band," Rowan moaned to me.

I knew what she meant. Linn had been on her best behaviour in front of Dad all through the movie and at the pizza place, but when he'd nipped off to pay the bill – while Rowan was trilling on excitedly about the band – Linn hadn't been able to resist sniping.

"They're thinking of calling themselves *what*?" she'd sneered, interrupting Rowan's enthusiastic gushing.

"Annihilator," Rowan had replied warily, knowing that Linn was going to sneer *whatever* their name happened to be.

"What's a nile hater?" Tor piped up.

"*Annihilator*?" Linn blurted out, blanking Tor's question. "What kind of *rubbish* name is that?"

Tor and I exchanged worried looks and both sucked hard on the straws of our milkshakes.

"It's a good one," Rowan had replied defensively. "And it's special, 'cause they're going to write it like ... like *this*."

Tor wriggled closer to see what Rowan was scribbling on the napkin with her eyeliner pencil.

"NNHLTR," Tor read out haltingly, sounding confused. "What's a 'NNHLTR'?"

"It's Annihilator, but with the vowels taken out," Rowan had enthused, opening her kohl-black eyes wide. "It's like a gimmick – isn't it clever? I think it'll be brilliant on posters. It'll *really* get them noticed!"

"Yeah, it'll get everyone thinking that they all failed their Key Stage One spelling tests!" Linn had snarled.

Rowan narrowed her eyes at Linn and looked like she wanted to do some annihilating herself. Luckily, Dad had come back to the table at that point, before Linn and Ro started stabbing each other with bread sticks or something.

"Maybe Linn needs cheering up," Tor suddenly announced, as he now lifted his feet off the ground and swung my and Ro's arms out of their sockets.

"Ooof ... I think that's what Dad tried to do, by taking us all out tonight, Tor," I replied, as the tendons in my arm pinged back into place.

"Maybe she needs a boyfriend," he surprised us

by saying next. "Like in the movie – that little dog fell in love with the big dog."

"I don't think snogging a dog would cheer Linn up," Rowan snickered.

"Nope – way too unhygienic!" I giggled. "It might get pawmarks on her top!"

"No!" Tor stomped. "I mean, Linn could go out with a *boy*!"

"Hmm … you'd have to be a pretty brave boy to go out with Linn," Rowan commented.

"True," I nodded. "God – it's hard to know what *would* cheer Linn up."

"A lobotomy?" Rowan suggested, opening her eyes wide and innocent.

"What's that?" asked Tor, whipping his head around to look at both of us in turn.

"It's … it's a kind of flower, Tor," I replied hastily, shooting a look over his head at Rowan to let her know that maybe we should keep a lid on the bitching in front of our little bro.

But our little bro had already fixed his attention on something else.

"Look!" he squealed, as we turned the corner into our road.

"Look at what?" I asked, squinting around.

There didn't seem to be anything out of the ordinary to see. No spaceships had landed in Palace

Heights Road while we'd been at the pictures; the Notting Hill Carnival weren't doing a dress rehearsal in the street; Tom Cruise hadn't arrived with a huge Hollywood location unit to shoot his new movie outside our house. All I could see was some people standing chatting on the pavement further down the road. Big wow.

"It's Rolf! And Winslet!" Tor yelped.

God, he was right. Those *did* look like our dogs, standing contentedly at the feet of ... of some people I couldn't make out yet. OK, this was getting weird; Rolf and Winslet should have been happily snoring indoors, sleeping off a mound of dog food and whatever cat food they'd managed to snaffle out of Colin & Co's bowls. How had they got out?

"And that's Michael and Harry, standing outside our gate!" Detective Tor continued.

"So it is!" murmured Rowan, recognizing our neighbours.

"And they're talking to some policemen!"

I glanced back at Dad and Linn, and saw from their worried expressions that they'd spotted what was going on, too.

Rolf and Winslet thought it was most excellent fun to see the entire Love clan sprint towards them at top speed, and set up a barrage of welcoming, deafening barks to greet us...

* * *

We'd been robbed. Well, kind of.

"This looks pretty bad. They've made a real mess of the place," said one of the two policemen, as he first peeked into the living room, then led the way through to the laundry-draped kitchen.

Rolf and Winslet padded along beside us, tongues dangling happily. So much for guard dogs – they were more like guard *blobs*. Instead of snarling at our intruders, they probably just sniffed them for snacks.

"Watch where you're stepping – there's broken glass there," the other policeman pointed out, as Rowan trod tentatively past the torn cereal packets on the floor and over towards the sink.

In the kitchen window, I noticed, there was a gaping hole where a pane of glass used to be, while shattered shards of glass glinted in the sink itself; this was where the burglars had got in. Sitting watching TV next door, our neighbours Michael and Harry had heard a second's worth of crash-bang-walloping going on, but hadn't been able to work out where it had come from. (Harry had been convinced the racket was actually on the telly. He and Michael were tuned in to *The Antiques Roadshow*, and Harry thought the smashing sound came courtesy of some hapless expert dropping some dear old lady's priceless family heirloom just out of sight of the cameras.)

Ten minutes later, Michael got up to make a cup of tea, and on the way to the kitchen he spotted – through the stained glass panel in his front door – a familiar silhouette hovering outside. Hearing some movement inside the house, the silhouette started barking madly, and Michael found himself licked to death by Rolf when he finally opened the front door. (Winslet shot straight past Michael's legs, her super-efficient Food Radar leading her directly to the kitchen, without passing Go, even though she'd never set paw in the house before.)

And that's when Michael had wandered next door and found *our* front door wide open – thanks to the burglars making their escape – and phoned the police.

"Sir, I'd appreciate it if you and your family could have a look around, so we can ascertain what's been taken," said the second policeman, talking to my stunned dad while gingerly stepping over Colin, who'd hopped into the kitchen to see what all the fuss was about.

I picked him up (Colin, that is – not the policeman) and hugged him hard, just to stop myself shaking. Partly, I was shaking through shock, but partly it was because I was feeling mildly hysterical and had this horrible feeling that I might start *giggling*, for God's sake. Honestly, the whole idea of strangers ransacking our lovely comfy house was so totally surreal that I wasn't sure whether I'd end up sniggering or sobbing in the next two minutes.

"Yes, but please don't touch or move anything, as we will be dusting for fingerprints soon," warned the first policeman, sounding exactly like a character off a cop show.

But despite what the police guys had just said, all five of us seemed rooted to the spot, too gob-smacked to do anything more than gawp around us. After what felt like for ever (and was probably more like a microsecond), Tor was first to break rank.

"The animals!" he squeaked, bolting for the stairs and dragging Dad by the hand with him.

"We'll check the bedrooms upstairs," Dad told the policemen, before following Tor to make sure that the burglars hadn't made off with their pockets stuffed full of indignant white mice, gerbils and stick insects.

"I'll check my own room," muttered Linn, scurrying close behind.

"Will we check the living room?" I asked Rowan, who shrugged a shaky shrug and followed me through on autopilot.

Our sunshine-yellow living room seemed suddenly alien, as if the burglars had stolen the very atmosphere of the place. OK, so all our pictures and knick-knacks and candles and stuff were still dotted over every available surface; magazines, newspapers and albums were scattered over the chairs and floor as usual; even our green-screened TV was still on – sound turned down – thanks to someone forgetting to switch it off before we went to the cinema… But it all felt *different* somehow.

"Are you all right?" I turned and asked Rowan, even though I was feeling pretty *not* all right myself.

Rowan nodded, her dark hair tumbling around her face. I think if anyone had said "Boo!" to her, she might have fainted on to the mussed-up rug on the floor (mussed up and wrinkled thanks to Rolf and the cats running around playing Sniff-Chase as usual, I bet).

"Here," I said, passing Colin to Rowan, since she seemed more in need of a cat-cuddle than me.

"Anything gone from here?" said a breathless Linn behind us in the doorway.

"Don't know," I replied, shaking myself into action and staring around the room. "What about upstairs?"

"Doesn't look like anything's gone from my

room, or yours," she panted, having thundered her way right to the top of the house and back down again. "I see they didn't take the TV..."

We all stared at the crap green screen.

"...or the video..." Linn continued.

We all stared at the dented, scratched video player, complete with a chewed tape dangling out of it that nobody had bothered to sort out since it had happened a couple of weeks before.

"...or the record player."

The centuries-old naff stereo sat with its layers of dust and greasy fingerprint smudges intact on the shelf above Mum and Dad's LPs, as per usual.

Aha.

I think the truth dawned on all three of us at the same time.

The mess the police had noticed? It wasn't down to heartless criminals ransacking our property; that was just standard Love family mess. (At least it was standard *weekend* mess – the place is always slightly better during the week, when Grandma's around. We're all too intimidated by her to be so messy, Monday to Friday.)

And I guess that, from a thief's point of view, all our arty junk and well-past-its-sell-by-date electrical gear was about as appealing as nicking soggy bread from the duck pond at Alexandra Palace.

"God, I'm so ashamed," Linn groaned, burying her face in her hands. "Even *burglars* think our house is too scuzzy to steal anything from!"

Hmm ... I'm not one to agree with Linn at the best of times, but maybe the Grouch Queen had a point.

Chapter 5

PLACE YOUR BETS (ON ROWAN LOSING)

It was hard concentrating on my homework, after our not-quite-burglary.

Actually ... I was probably just using that as an excuse.

After all, by Monday night, I was well and truly wobble-free about the whole thing. For a start, when the police finally left us on Sunday night (trying not to smirk when Dad explained that the boxes littering the kitchen floor were actually an art project and not the work of a crazed, drugged-up vandal), Grandma had turned up to dish out practical comfort and vast helpings of ice-cream.

And both those things really sorted us out: ice-cream, because it's, well, ice-cream (and totally brilliant), and Grandma, well, because she's so unruffle-able. Honestly, if she'd been on the *Titanic* when it was going down, she'd have tutted at everyone screaming and panicking. And on Sunday night, her calmness in the face of our not-quite-burglary quickly rubbed off on us all.

("Never mind! No harm done! Now, who's for another helping?")

Secondly, I'd stopped feeling wobbly after I'd talked it all out with my mates the next day. I turned into a bit of a celebrity at school, recounting the not-quite-drama of our not-quite-burglary to all my friends. And I was comforted when Jen pointed out that every robber in the London area would probably have heard by now that it wasn't worth their while *ever* trying to break into 28 Palace Heights Road.

And hoorah to that.

Anyway, back to the homework I didn't seem able to concentrate on. If I couldn't blame burglars, then I was going to have to give in and get on with it. But I'd just brushed a cat that wasn't Colin off my History book – all ready to make a start – when my attention was grabbed by one Very Peculiar Noise coming from somewhere downstairs.

"What's that, puss?" I asked the cat that wasn't Colin, who – sensing I was about to get up and investigate – settled itself back on my warm History book.

As I padded down the attic stairs to the first-floor landing, I saw Winslet padding up from the hallway, obviously just as intrigued as I was by the

Very Peculiar Noise. Which was actually more of a Very Peculiar *Whine*.

"Where's it coming from, Winnie?" I whispered.

Winslet, being Winslet, completely ignored me and headed straight to the source of the noise: Rowan's room. Standing on her short, hairy back legs, our determined dog used the weight of her abnormally long, hairy body to force the door open. She then trotted in and stood staring at my sister, who was perched on her bed with an aura of twinkly fairy-lights sparkling behind her.

Oh, yes – the Very Peculiar Whine was coming directly out of Rowan's mouth.

"What are you doing?" I asked my slightly older, slightly madder sister as I wandered in and planted myself in her plastic blow-up chair.

"Singing!" Rowan batted her long eyelashes at me. "What did you think I was doing?"

"I dunno," I shrugged, squelching myself around to get comfy. "From the noise, I thought Tor had brought home a sick whale or something."

"Very funny," Rowan rolled her eyes.

Now that Ro's whale song had stopped, Winslet relaxed, flopped her doggy self down on to the faded bedroom carpet and began distractedly chewing on the nearest available object, which happened to be a plastic hairbrush.

"So what were you – ahem – singing?" I grinned at my sister.

"This," she replied, holding up a pad with scribbled lyrics on it. "I'm trying to write something for Chazza's band."

"What, like a *song*?" I said stupidly, peering at the lyrics, which I couldn't make out, since Ro's handwriting looks like a whole bunch of spiders playing Tag.

"Yeah, like a *song*," Rowan laughed.

"What for?" I asked, stretching over and grabbing the pad from her.

"For a bet," she replied.

"Huh?" I glanced up sharply at her.

"For a bet," she repeated. "Chazza's band have got their first gigs coming up, and he says they really need to get a slow, moody song in their set, but all the lads have been able to write so far is noisy, loud stuff."

"So?" I frowned, wondering what any of that had to do with her.

"So, I bet him *I* could write something," Ro explained. "And he took me up on it. He's given me a week to come up with a song."

I glanced down at the pad I was holding and read what she'd scribbled so far.

" '*Baby, it's true / I'm a little bit blue / 'Cause I*

want you / Ooooooh…'," I read out aloud from the page.

Hmm.

"What do you think? It's rubbish, isn't it?" Rowan blurted out, disarming me with her honesty.

OK, so I might have made the wisecrack about the whale yodelling, but I knew it would be too mean to agree with Rowan about the quality of her lyrics. Even if she was right about them being rubbish.

"Well, maybe the words aren't quite *moody* enough, if that's what you were going for," I muttered, hoping I sounded like I was giving constructive criticism.

Hearing the thrash-metal guitar screeching on Chazza's demo the day before, I didn't think his band was going to be too thrilled with a slushy, gushy love song. Especially a *rubbish* slushy, gushy love song.

"Well, I didn't think Chazza would actually take me up on the bet!" Rowan shrugged, looking slightly panicky around the edges.

"Hold on – these are just the lyrics," I said, wafting the spider-scrawled page around. "Let me hear the tune again."

"You want me to sing it?" Ro blinked at me.

"Yeah," I nodded, trying to come across all

encouraging, and hoping Rowan's whining would sound more tuneful close up than it had when I was outside her bedroom door.

(Dream on…)

"Babeeee, it's truuuuuue…"

Winslet's ears pricked up, and she stopped chewing the mangled fragments of hairbrush between her teeth.

"I'm a little bit bluuuuue…"

Winslet sat up, fixed her beady eyes on my warbling sister, and tilted her floppy-eared head from side to side in confusion.

"'Cause I want yoooooooo…"

Winslet started to growl softly.

"Oooooohhhhh!"

"AAAhowwwwWHOOOOOOOOOOOOOOOO!" Winslet suddenly joined in on backing vocals.

Er – this song thing: to me, it looked like this was one bet that Rowan was in *serious* danger of losing…

Chapter 6

(BITTER)SWEET INSPIRATION

It was Wednesday night, i.e. Rowan's song deadline was two days closer. Which wasn't a problem, since she'd already finished writing it.

Yeah, *right*.

"What am I going to do?" Rowan moaned, as she whirled a tea towel over the dripping plate I'd just handed her, and stared soulfully out of the new pane of glass in the kitchen window. "I can't think of a tune ... I can't think of any decent lyrics..."

"What about: *'I can't write songs and my cooking pongs'*," came a sarky suggestion courtesy of Linn, who was busying herself wiping the table and listening in to my and Rowan's conversation.

"What about: *'Shut up, or I'll strangle you with this tea towel'*," Rowan hissed, *just* loud enough for me to hear.

"It doesn't rhyme," I whispered back, grinning cheekily, which at least got Rowan smiling. "Anyway, just ignore her."

Rowan nodded at my whispered advice. Grandma had left for the evening and Dad would be heading off out soon to his (urgh) line-dancing class, so we were both in danger of suffering the Wrath of Linn, undefended. Oh, yes – despite family-bonding moments like nearly being burgled, Linn's lousy mood was dragging on and on and *on* (worse luck), and Rowan and I had decided that the best way to deal with it was to more or less ignore her, since everything we did and said seemed to irritate her, including *breathing*.

"Don't know what you're bothering to try and write a song for anyway, Ro," Linn carried on carping in the background. "It's not like anyone will ever get the chance to *hear* it."

"And why not?" Rowan snapped, forgetting my advice in a nanosecond, now that Linn's words were wriggling under her skin.

"Well, face it," Linn shrugged. "No one's *seriously* going to listen to Chazza's band play!"

"For *your* information, *Linnhe*," Rowan replied huffily, "Annihilator—"

"Isn't that 'Nnhtlr'?" I grunted, as a stupid joke to try and lighten the rapidly darkening atmosphere. Like anyone *noticed*.

"– are doing a warm-up gig on Friday at a pub in Holloway," Rowan continued, staring daggers at

Linn, "and they're headlining at the Student Union in a couple of weeks' time!"

"*Head*lining?!" Linn laughed dryly. "Well, that should be fun for the two people and a dog that'll turn up to watch them!"

I tell you, I've never been so glad to hear a doorbell ring. Whether it was someone trying to tell me and my family about the joy of the Bible or sell us dusters, I didn't care. I'd happily talk about Jesus and his many miracles or examine a selection of scouring pads for an hour rather than stay in the kitchen for *one* more minute while Linn and Rowan were squaring up for a hissy fit.

"Billy! It's you! Brilliant!" I grinned, surprising my buddy with my enthusiasm as soon as I opened the front door. "Come in!"

I pulled Billy into the hall with one hand and grabbed his bike from him with the other, propping it up against the wall (and nearly up against Rolf's head, if he hadn't woken up and lolloped off as fast as he did).

"It's only Billy!" I told Dad, sticking my head around the living-room door.

"Cool!" Dad turned and nodded, wriggling his arm free from the huge volume of weight it was under and giving me a quick thumbs-up. (It's funny that there's a huge sofa, another armchair and a beanbag in that room, but Tor, Winslet and Colin were all vying for space on top of Dad and the chair he was sitting on.)

"Hi, Mr Love!" Billy said politely, attempting to put in an appearance at the living-room door, but I was already bounding up the stairs, dragging him with me by the hood of his grey Ellesse top.

"So what's new?" I asked Billy, as I took two-at-a-time steps towards the attic and my bedroom.

"Nothing much," Billy shrugged, swirling his baseball cap around so that the peak covered his face from my scrutiny.

"Were you just bored or something?"

It wasn't as if I *minded* Billy coming to see me through sheer boredom. After all, it was his *usual* reason for cycling uninvited over the hill, past the Palace and through the park towards my house. And it's quite flattering when you think about it: it must mean he thinks I'm interesting.

Then again, maybe hanging out with me is just *marginally* less boring for Billy than being bored on his own...

"Nah, I'm not bored exactly," Billy muttered, as he followed me into my room, which was warm, bright and cosy as the evening sunshine streamed in through the little window.

Two cats that weren't Colin were making the

most of the end-of-the-day rays, I noticed. Frankie was on my bed, lying on his back in a shaft of light, with his legs (and wonky tail) splayed out around him, looking slightly dead but very contented. Also on the bed, but looking much more alive, was Derek, who was amusing himself by fixing his crossed eyes on drifting dust particles and trying to pounce on them.

"Well, it's not been too boring round here at the moment!" I told Billy, as I sat myself down on the bed and started stroking Frankie, just to make sure he did have a pulse.

"Prrp!"

A pulse *and* a voice – yep, he was alive.

"Yeah? Heard any more about the burglars?" Billy asked distractedly, as he walked over to the window and gazed out at the view.

I frowned to myself – was something up with Billy? Let's face it: he's not really a gazing-at-views kind of boy. (Actually, I find boys in general aren't into gazing at views, unless that view happens to be twenty centimetres in front of their noses on a PlayStation.)

"Those creeps? Nope," I shook my head, although Billy wasn't looking at me to see that. "It's just that it's been a bit lively with Linn and Rowan the last couple of days."

I paused, giving Billy a chance to say, "How come?" Only he didn't; he just kept gazing out of the window, his hands shoved deep down in the pockets of his khaki skate shorts.

"Linn's still in one of her moodies where she hates her life and hopes she's going to be claimed as the long-lost daughter of a zillionaire, world-famous interior designer or something –"

Not a grin, not a reaction from my best mate. Weird.

"– and Rowan's still trying to come up with a song to win this bet with Chazza, only she can't think of anything to write," I chattered on, while studying Billy's back and wondering what the score was with him. "I was thinking I should maybe give her a hand – if she splits the money with me. What do you reckon?"

I gave Billy a moment to answer me, and when he didn't, I put on a dumb, deep voice and answered myself.

"Good idea!" I boomed, in a truly crap impersonation of Billy. "Thought of any brilliant ideas, Ally?"

The reaction from Billy? There wasn't one.

"*Well*, Billy, I thought it *could* be something about people rubbing each other up the wrong way – you know, like Ro and Linn," I blabbed on, reverting back to my own voice. "Or maybe it should be about people invading your space, like those super-creepy burglars. Both of those might work as ideas for songs. But then, it could still be a love song, too, only one with a twist to it. Just as long as it's not some corny, barfy 'Ooh, baby' thing; y'know, the type Boyzone used to—"

"She dumped me."

"Excuse me?" I asked, jumping – along with a startled Derek – as Billy spun around and spoke all of a sudden.

"She dumped me," Billy repeated, with a short, sharp shrug.

"'She Dumped Me'… yeah, that's OK, I s'pose," I mused, not wild about the song title Billy had suggested but just happy to have him snap out of his view-gazing coma and talk to me.

"No! I mean, she *dumped* me, Ally!" Billy suddenly gushed. "Anita's dumped me!"

"Oh, my God! Poor Billy! When did all this happen? Tonight?"

"Nope," I replied, from the comfort of Ro's squashy blow-up chair. "Two weeks ago."

"And he never *told* you!" Rowan gasped, slapping her purple nail-varnished hands theatrically against her chest, covering up the big butterfly emblazoned on her number one favourite T-shirt.

"He was too embarrassed to say anything to me. *Or* anyone else," I explained, still reeling from Billy's confession half an hour ago.

When he blurted it all out – in particular, the bit about keeping the dumping secret for so long – I hadn't known whether to laugh, commiserate with him or tell him he was an idiot, so I did all three, and gave the big geek a hug into the bargain. Honestly, can you imagine keeping devastating news like that to yourself? Billy must have been *so* miserable the last couple of weeks. No wonder he'd gone a bit funny on us in Camden on Saturday, when Sandie was teasing him about Anita...

"*Poor* Billy!" Rowan muttered again, her eyes suddenly looking as twinkly as the fairy lights draped all around her room.

I knew Rowan would be understanding about Billy's confession, but I wished she wouldn't do the twinkly-eyed bit – I was still feeling a little goosebumpy about the whole thing myself.

"Anita told him she really liked him ... but not enough," I explained.

Rowan sighed a wistful sigh at my words.

"Not enough..." she repeated, slowly, poetically.

I took a sharp breath – what Rowan had just done was like a *sign*. The thing was, I hadn't just trawled up Billy's misery with her because I knew she'd be sympathetic; I was splurging it to her for another reason entirely.

"Listen, don't you think there's maybe a *song* idea in what happened with Billy?" I suggested to her, trying to lean forward to emphasize my point but finding that very, very hard to do in a semi-deflated inflatable chair.

"Wow!" Rowan gasped for the second time in less than a minute. "*Yes!* Spurned love! And a spurned love that hurts so much you can't *stand* to tell *anyone* about it!"

"Good, isn't it?" I grinned, getting caught up in Rowan's enthusiasm and forgetting the sad source of my inspiration for a second. "It's like a loser's love song. And it could be called 'Not Enough'."

Rowan's eyes were twinkling again, but with excitement instead of sorry-for-Billy tears.

"That's *great*, Ally!" she bubbled. "Chazza and the boys will *love* that idea!"

Yes! Eighteen-year-old boys are going to love me! I screamed out loud inside my head. *Er ... well, at least they're going to love my idea for a quirky, moody, slow song!*

"Ally, we've *got* to work on this together – please say yes! I can't do it on my own, and you're fantastic with words and everything!" Rowan begged me.

"OK," I said casually, while my entire insides were fainting with happiness. I'd only been joking with Billy when I'd mentioned helping Ro with her songwriting attempts.

"Hey – I've had an idea!" trilled Rowan. "Ally, you should come along to the pub on Friday and see the band for yourself. That way, it would make it easier to write with them in mind!"

Good idea.

Smart idea, in fact.

That's if Rowan hadn't been forgetting one *teeny*-tiny detail...

Excuse me if I've got this wrong, but since *when* have thirteen year olds officially been allowed into sweaty, crowded bars on Friday nights?

Chapter 7

EARPLUGS AT THE READY

My outfit: light-grey fitted T-shirt; dark-grey combats; grey and white trainers. Nice, but all guaranteed to make me fade into the background this Friday night. I *hoped*.

Rowan's outfit: a bright pink, mandarin-collared, flower-embroidered genuine Chinese silk dress (bought not in China, but for £3.50 from the Cancer Research shop in Crouch End); a denim jacket customized with a pink sequin heart sewn on the back; purple silk Indian mules (with sequins, natch); and a pink lily hairgrip the size of a satellite dish (nearly). Nice, but all guaranteed to show me up *big* time this Friday night.

Don't get me wrong; I was dead excited at the idea of going out with my older sister – i.e. not just out to the shops or out to Park Road swimming pool or something, but properly *out* out. (Rowan might only be fifteen, but her social life is seriously groovy, since she hangs out with the likes of Von and Chazza, both eighteen years old and unspeakably cool.) And, at last, I was going to be part of that, even if I was so nervous I felt just a little bit like barfing. It was just that no matter how many times Rowan told me it would be fine, I was still quietly flipping out at the idea of going into a pub under age.

Still, it was some small comfort to know that all my mates were dead jealous...

"So, we're off out, then," Rowan announced, a vision of pinkly pink in the living room, while I stood pale-grey and wan beside her.

"Well, have a great time, girls," said Dad, bending down to study the TV at close quarters as he spoke.

"Ally will be fine. She'll be with me and Von the whole time. We'll look after her."

"Yes, Ro, I know you will," Dad nodded, as he twiddled knobs he didn't know how to work in an effort to make the screen slightly less green. "You've told me already."

"And the band have cleared it with the pub manager – as long as we sit at the side of the stage and Ally doesn't drink, then he doesn't have a problem with her being there."

"Well, if *he* doesn't, *I* don't," said Dad, frowning as a knob came off in his hand.

"The band will only be on stage for about an hour, and I'll take Ally home straight after."

"Ro, you don't have to try so hard to convince me!" Dad laughed, straightening up and sticking the knob on the top of the fireplace for safe-keeping, till he got around to fixing it (i.e. it would stay on the fireplace gathering dust for *months*). "I *know* this is a one-off; I *know* this is research because you want to write a song for the band; and I said that I *know* I can rely on you – *and* Ally. I have every faith in both of you."

He gave me a wink, and started shooing us out of the door, hurrying us off to have fun.

What a brilliant, open-minded, trusting dad to have...

When I thought about it, Rowan's assurances to Dad were pretty screwy, really, considering:

a) That it wasn't just *me* who was under age: Ro wasn't exactly the right side of eighteen herself.

b) She'd made them all up.

Yep, after going out of her way to tell Dad (and me) that everything would be fine, Rowan started flipping out as soon as we got in sight of the pub – which made me feel fantastically confident.

Not.

"Look at that!" said Von, who'd just met us off the bus. "The band's name, see? 'NNHLTR – tonight at 8 p.m.'"

"Oh, God!" Rowan gasped, but not at the chalk-board sign sitting on the pavement outside the pub, advertising the gig. "They've got a bouncer on the door! We'll never get Ally in!"

"Um ... I thought you said Chazza had sorted things out with the manager?" I pointed out, feeling pterodactyl-sized butterflies suddenly start flapping their way around my stomach.

"Ha!" snorted Von, blanking me (as usual) and gazing directly at Rowan through her curtain of long, straight black hair. "Chazza sorting stuff out? I don't *think* so! He can't sort out his *laundry*!"

"Rowan?" I bleated, hoping my sister was about to reassure me and send the pterodactyls on their way.

But Rowan just bit her lip and hauled me into a shop doorway.

"I just *said* that stuff to convince Dad it'd be OK, Ally," she shrugged apologetically at me. "Von – can you put some more make-up on Ally to make her look older?"

"*You* do it, Ro, and I'll phone Chazza and see if he can get us in through the back way or some-thing," Von sighed irritably, as she rooted around in her bag for her mobile. "And get rid of that ponytail – it makes her look about twelve."

The stubby ponytail was mine; the "her" was

me, of course. Well, I'd only stopped being twelve a few months earlier, so what did Von expect? And what was wrong with looking twelve or thirteen anyway? Snotty moo – just 'cause *she* was miffed at Rowan bringing me along and complicating her night out.

"Listen, I don't want to do this any more," I protested, as Rowan backed me into the corner of the doorway and started daubing blusher on my cheeks.

Too *right* I didn't want to do it any more. On top of everything else, Von was suddenly making me feel about as welcome as chickenpox.

"But you've *got* to see the band play!" Rowan insisted, while coming at me with some dark-purple eyeshadow.

(Mmm, wanna look like you've gone ten rounds with Mike Tyson and come out with two black eyes? No *thank* you...)

"But I *could* just listen to that demo tape Chazza brought round the other day!" I suggested, ducking away from the advancing make-up brush. "I don't actually need to *see* them to help you write the –"

I didn't get to say the word "song"; Rowan stopped me by widening her eyes to bush-baby proportions then nodding her head in the direction of Von, who was presently (reluctantly) hatching a plan with Chazza on the phone to sneak us inside, commando-style.

Aha – it seemed that Rowan hadn't let Von in on the fact that I was going to be helping her win the bet with Chazza. I suppose if Von or anyone in the band knew a thirteen year old had anything to do with the song they'd have got a total downer on it straight away.

Just like I suddenly had a total downer on tonight…

"Look," I pleaded, trying my best to wriggle past Rowan, "let me go – I'm going home."

"No! Please stay, Ally Pally!" said Rowan, holding on to my arm. "It'll be fantastic – honest it will!"

With Rowan's track record for honesty that evening, I should have just leapt on the nearest No. 91 bus and spent the night in front of the green telly with Dad and Tor. But somehow I let her persuade me – probably because I knew that Billy, Sandie, Kyra and the rest of my friends would *kill* me if I didn't come back to them with tales of rock-star wildness…

Rock-star scuzziness, more like. And there was nothing starry about the pub (a scruffy, smelly dump) or the audience (a bunch of grungy, grunting lads). There was nothing starry about the band, either (another bunch of grungy, grunting lads, who all looked like clones of Chazza). After being smuggled through the wee-scented back alley and hidden away at a table in a dark corner beside the wee-scented gents' toilets, I'd sat and watched the well-named Annihilator (sorry, NNHLTR) murder a whole *bunch* of songs.

"Is the drummer *meant* to be speeding up and slowing down?" I yelled into Rowan's ear, as the band lurched loudly into yet another tune-free track (the last one – phew).

"I don't *think* so," Rowan grimaced.

"And who told that guy he could sing?" I barked, staring up at the cocky-looking poser in the ripped T-shirt and jeans hogging the mike and honking like a goose with asthma.

"Don't know, but he shouldn't have believed them!" Rowan giggled back.

He really thought he was something, that lad; a blindfolded goat could tell he fancied himself as God's gift to women and indie music. It was just the way he snarled and swaggered around the stage, coming across like Liam Gallagher trying to do a Chippendales routine. Well, some of the studenty girls in the audience might have been eyeing him up, but this love god wasn't doing it for either of the Love girls.

"What did you say his name was, Ro?" I asked her, remembering it was something suitably pretentious.

"It's Q, as in Q the letter," replied Rowan, wincing as the drummer accidentally kicked over his cymbals and they went crashing on to Chazza's foot.

Poor Rowan. From the look on her face as she watched Chazza limp and swear his way through the last bars of the song, you could tell she was definitely pretty disappointed that her friend's first gig was such *pants*. Thank goodness Linn wasn't around to gloat.

Ever heard the phrase "famous last words"...?

"*Well,*" came a familiar voice behind us, just after Q grunted the band's goodbyes and they all shuffled off to the bar. "That was ... *lousy.*"

Rowan and I and even Von spun round in our seats, and focused on the two faces looming over us. One of those faces was (in my eyes) adorable, while the other was ... Linn's.

"Uh, hi, Ally," Alfie nodded his beautiful, cropped blond head casually at me (ooh, just scoop me up off the floor, someone).

Meanwhile, Rowan positively *glowered* up at Linn.

"What are *you* doing here?!" Rowan demanded,

feeling her space well and truly invaded by our big, bossy sister.

"Hi!" I mouthed back at Alfie, crossing my fingers under the table that I didn't look too much of a tarted-up troll in the lipstick and eye make-up Rowan had made me wear.

"We're on our way to a party around the corner," Linn shrugged, "and Dad asked me to pop in here and see that Ally was OK."

Um, *what* was I saying earlier about my brilliant, open-minded, trusting dad...?

"Of *course* she's OK!" Rowan huffed.

"Of course I'm OK!" I chipped in, mortified to think that Alfie had been dragged in here to check on my welfare too.

"Fine!" said Linn, indifferently. "Well, that's what he wanted me to check!"

"Fine!" Rowan stated loudly, her chair screeching as she stood up. "Von, you can stay if you want, but I'd better take Ally home *right* now, since Dad *obviously* doesn't trust me to look after her!"

Wow – what an all-round rubbish evening. It started with me being forced to do a very bad, very unconvincing impression of an eighteen year old, and now I felt like some tiny kid, being taken home 'cause it was way past my bedtime.

And in front of Alfie, too. Oh, the humiliation.

Guess this wasn't the night he was going to find himself falling helplessly, hopelessly in love with me, then...

Chapter (8)

NO THANK Q...

"There you go, girls!" Dad smiled nervously, sticking the tray down on the rug. "Just a little something to keep you going while you're working!"

The "work" was the song Ro and I were struggling to write (we were still giving it a go – even after Friday – since Chazza had assured Rowan that Annihilator's spectacularly rubbish performance was down to nerves and lack of practice). The "little something" was two mugs of hot chocolate and what looked like a whole packet of Jaffa Cakes on a plate.

"Thanks, Dad!" I smiled up at him.

"No problem! Just yell if you need anything else!" he beamed, backing gingerly out of my bedroom door, while at the same time expertly scooping up Winslet as she tried to zoom into the room with her nose aimed at the biscuits like an Exocet missile.

"Aw, isn't he sweet!" Rowan sighed softly as the

door clicked shut and we heard Dad's Dr Marten's pound down the stairs (with an accompanying whimper from a protesting Winslet).

"He's trying *so* hard, isn't he?" I whispered back, through a mouthful of Jaffa Cake.

Dad had been trying hard since Friday night, when Rowan tearfully accused him of lying over the matter of trust (which was a bit much, really, considering the fibbing *she*'d done). Dad kept saying sorry and explained that he didn't *mean* to be overprotective; the trouble is, once Rowan switches on the sniffles, it's very hard to get her to stop.

"Oh, Ally, and I've upset you too!" he'd said, spotting my red-rimmed eyes and leaving Ro for a second to give me a hug.

Actually, I felt like a big, fat faker when he did that. Yeah, I was upset about Alfie thinking I was just some dumb kid (hey, what's new?), but the *real* reason my eyes were red-rimmed was because the millisecond me and Rowan had arrived home, I'd zapped upstairs to the bathroom and used a *bit* too much soap to scrub off the make-up on my face before Dad spotted it.

Anyway, all three of us ended up having a hug (with Rolf trying to join in, since it looked like fun), and made up over late-night tea and toast (*also* with Rolf). Over the next couple of days, Dad had been super-sweet to us, even though I felt that the whole *hiccup* wasn't really all his fault.

"Do you think Mum would be strict with us, if she was here?" Rowan mused, flicking biscuit crumbs off the scribbled lyrics for "Not Enough".

"But she was *never* strict," I answered her, remembering how silly and scatty and soft our mother was with us.

"Yeah, but we weren't teenagers back then," Ro pointed out. "We were just kids, doing kids' stuff. I mean, apart from him asking Linn to spy on us on Friday, Dad's always really cool about what we do. But maybe Mum would be more, y'know, *angsty* about us going out at night and everything. If she was *here*, I mean."

If she was here… How often had we all said that over the past four years?

"Linn would know," I pointed out. "She was a teenager when Mum left. *She* was thirteen, same as I am now."

A frizzle of a some strange feeling shot up and down my spine when I said that. How weird.

"We could ask her," said Rowan, raising her eyebrows at me questioningly.

We probably could.

After seven long, *long* days, Linn's black cloud of

gloom had finally floated off into the horizon this weekend, leaving the smiling, pleasant version of Linn we all looked forward to seeing. Who knew what hormonal wind had blown the bad mood away; and frankly, who *cared*. Just as long as life was more pleasant (i.e. *Linn* was more pleasant), none of the rest of us was going to complain.

"Come on, then," I said, scrambling to my feet.

I know we had a song to write, but if there's one thing me and both my sisters like doing, it's having an excuse to talk about Mum – it makes it feel like she's just that little bit less far away.

Rowan struggled to get up and follow me, getting herself tangled up in her ratty old kimono dressing gown (serves her right for not getting out of her pyjamas all day).

"I'm coming!" she called after me, as I padded along the attic landing and tapped at Linn's bedroom door.

"Is she there?" asked Ro.

"Doesn't sound like it," I replied, tapping at the door again. "Linn?"

"Listen," Ro frowned, tilting her head so that the tangle of hair she'd bundled up on her head with a scrunchie started slipping sideways. "That's her mobile ringing in there!"

So it was – she had some Destiny's Child track

as her ring tone. It was amazing that Linn had left the house without her precious phone; since she'd treated herself to it with the wages from her Saturday job, that thing had been practically superglued to the side of her head, gently micro-waving her brain with electric currents (according to my disapproving gran).

"*LINN* – are you down there?" I bellowed, leaning over the bannister and staring all the way past the first-floor landing to the ground floor hallway. "It's your *PHONE*!"

"SHE'S OUT!" Tor yelled back, staring up at me, while Rolf stood beside him with a large white bandage tied round his middle. Looked like Tor was playing *Animal Hospital* again…

"She's out," I turned and repeated to my sister, although Ro had to have heard. "She must have forgotten to take her phone with her."

Destiny's Child trilled on softly in the background.

"Should we answer it?" Rowan grimaced at me.

Hmm. Linn was only *just* speaking to us again. Dare we stray into her room, even with the best of intentions?

"It goes on to the message-answering-service thingy, doesn't it?" I asked her, trying to remember how my friends' mobile phones worked.

"It's supposed to. But it's ringing for an awfully long time…"

We stared at each other, reading each other's minds. What would wind Linn up most – knowing we'd trespassed in the Temple of Linn without permission, or finding out we hadn't taken what could be a VIC (Very Important Call)?

"We should answer it," said Rowan, opening the door and pushing *me* inside, I noticed.

Linn's silver mobile was easy to spot, lying right in the middle of the whiter-than-white duvet cover.

"*You* answer it!" I grinned, scooping up the mobile and chucking it at Rowan, who was hovering in the doorway.

Ro did a great catch, her hands appearing from the depths of her baggy kimono sleeves in a flash.

"Hello?" she said smoothly, then stuck her tongue out at me. "No, she's not here. Can I take a message?"

It's a boy! she mouthed excitedly at me, pointing frantically to the phone.

Ooh! Who could this be? Not Alfie, that was for sure – Ro would have recognized his slow drawl straight away.

"You want to meet her at eight tonight, instead of half-seven," said Rowan, obviously repeating what the boy had just said, and obviously doing it for *my* benefit.

I held my breath – to stop myself giggling and setting Ro off.

Hey, it looked like Linn had a date! Was this the reason she'd turned into a little ray of sunshine over the weekend? Had she met someone cute at that party she'd gone to on Friday night?

"Um, so sorry – what's your name?" Rowan asked, glancing at me and then glancing away before the giggles got the better of her too.

I was biting my thumb by now, gagging to laugh and desperate to find out who Linn's secret admirer was. Staring at Ro's face in anticipation, the last thing I expected was for her smile to slip away so instantly.

"OK! I'll tell her! Bye!" she said hurriedly, then slammed her thumb on the End Call button.

"What? Who was it?" I asked her.

"Q!"

"What? That big-headed guy in Chazza's band?" I squeaked, though who knows why I was asking. I mean, how many other Qs are there in the world? Who else would be so pretentious to name themselves after one letter of the alphabet?

"*Linn* is seeing Q?" Rowan blinked.

Ro and I just stood and stared at each other.

The only thing intruding on our shocked silence was the snuffling sound of Winslet wolfing down Jaffa Cakes in my room next door...

Chapter 9

THE LEANING TOWER OF CARROT

"Why aren't you eating your carrots?" Grandma frowned at Tor across the table.

"I am!" said Tor indignantly, although that wasn't exactly true. Instead of putting them anywhere near his mouth, Tor had piled up his slices of carrot into a Leaning Tower of ... well, *Carrot* at the side of his glass of milk.

Grandma narrowed her eyes at him, knowing he was up to something, but said no more. Strange things are always happening to Tor's food, which is regularly transformed into edible sculptures before he gets around to stuffing his face with it. For example: this Monday night, his corn on the cob had been standing upright – representing the space rocket *Discovery* – in a mound of fluffy mashed potato, which represented the billows of white smoke at the rocket's launch. As if you hadn't guessed that already.

"Oh, I meant to ask – how did Charles's show go?" Grandma asked, changing the subject and helping herself to another dollop of mashed potato.

There are many (many) things my gran disapproves of, and one of those is "stupid" nicknames. So in Grandma's book, Chazza is *always* Charles – even if no one else knows him as that. Including my sister. Blissfully unaware that Grandma was talking to her, Rowan carried on scrutinizing the end of one of her plaits for split ends, while with her other hand she speared peas on to her fork.

"Ro!" I said sharply. "Grandma's asking how Chazza's gig went on Friday!"

"Oh!" Ro perked up, now that I'd interpreted for her. "It was OK! Well, it was pretty bad, wasn't it, Ally?"

"You mean, *Linn*," Dad laughed a little too hard. "*Linn* went to the gig with you, didn't she?"

Rowan stared quizzically at him, then finally got the message.

"Oh, yes! Yes, *course* I meant Linn!" she corrected herself, realizing the boob she'd made.

I crossed my fingers (which make it kind of *tricky* to hold a fork, actually) and hoped Grandma hadn't spotted it.

(Another thing on Grandma's Disapproval List is the idea of any of us kids going into "licensed premises". She's reluctantly accepted that both

Linn and Rowan *do* go to over-eighteen places from time to time, but I think it's safe to say that she'd definitely flip out at the notion of *me* being in a pub. As Dad knew only too well, which is why he was just as desperate as we were to keep quiet about the Annihilator do.)

"The gig wasn't all *that* bad," Linn shrugged, keeping her eyes fixed on her food.

My eyes flickered over to Rowan, who gave me a knowing grin in return.

"*Really*, Linnhe?" said Ro, raising her eyebrows at our pink-cheeked big sister. "*That's* funny! I could have *sworn* you said they were 'lousy' before. What *could* have made you change your mind?"

Ouch. It was impossible not to wince under the weight of all that sarcasm.

"Very funny, Ro!" Linn flushed. "I know what you're getting at, but I *told* you last night when you gave me my phone message: Q is just a friend, OK?"

"Since when?" Rowan retorted. "You'd never set eyes on him before Friday!"

"Who's this?" frowned Grandma, interrupting the brewing bubble of tension building between my sisters. "Who are you talking about?"

"Q," Rowan jumped in before Linn could. "He's the singer in Chazza's band."

"Q?" repeated Tor, wrinkling his nose up.

"How do you spell that?" Grandma asked warily.

"Just ... Q," Linn said defensively. "Like in the letter."

"That's not a name!" Grandma insisted. "What's his *proper* name?"

"I don't know," Linn replied, standing up and agitatedly starting to clear away the dishes, even though some of us were still eating.

"Well, that was lovely!" Dad tried to enthuse, as he longingly watched his half-finished tea being swept away from under his nose.

"Can I go, Dad?" Rowan asked to be excused, above the noise of Linn clattering dishes in the sink.

"Sure," Dad nodded, without asking where she was off to.

I think he was too worried that we'd be spending the night supergluing the crockery back together, the way Linn was treating them with such brute force...

I knew where Rowan was off to; she was going to meet Chazza for a coffee and a catch-up.

Her visit had a dual purpose: first, she planned on showing him the song that she (i.e. *we*) had spent the day before writing; and secondly, she was going to pump Chazza for information about what the deal was with Linn and Q, since Linn was being such a spoilsport and refusing to spill the beans.

Me? Well, I had a totally *thrilling* Monday night planned.

Let's see ... *drying* the dishes, *helping* Tor clean out the rabbit hutch, *watching* Tor feed Cilla & Co the Leaning Tower of Carrot he'd smuggled out (more exciting for them than normal carrots, apparently, since they were covered in gravy). And now was the most exciting part of the whole evening, if you didn't count the splinter I'd just got in my bum.

"Look!" said Tor, his face a picture of rapture and enthusiasm.

"Wow!" I said, as I sat crossed-legged in the garden shed (hence the splinter) and watched Tor spill a pile of bin-worthy rubbish out of a cardboard box and on to the floor.

These junk treasures were what he and his mate Freddie had collected from their families to flog at a charity table sale the boys planned to have outside our house next weekend. It was for a great cause: the local Hamster Rescue Association. Tor had heard about it from Michael the vet next door, who'd told him that some batty old woman (my words, not Michael's) had come into the surgery and asked to put a notice up about the Association. Tor got very excited when he heard that they needed hamster foster homes, but when Dad gently but firmly said no, Tor turned his attention to the idea of becoming a hamster fund-raiser.

"There's this, this, and *this*!" he said, holding up a half-full bottle of bubble bath, a one-legged Sindy and an ancient, dog-eared copy of *Sugar* magazine in quick succession.

"That's brilliant, Tor!" I nodded, picking up a packet of felt pens that looked suspiciously dried-out. "You'll get *lots* of money for this stuff!"

"Do you think?" asked my wide-eyed little brother.

"Duh – *no*!" was the obvious answer, but he wasn't going to hear it from me.

Instead, what he *did* hear was a polite tapping at the shed door (and a telltale tinkling of bracelets), followed by a screech as the wooden door was pulled open.

"Can I come in?" Rowan grinned, stepping in and crouching down beside the two of us. "So, what are you doing? Clearing out the shed or something?"

"No!" I jumped in. "This is the stuff for Tor's charity sale!"

"Ah, of course!" muttered Rowan. "Still want

me to make you a special sign for your table, Tor?"

"Yes, please," he nodded, not seeming to have noticed her slight on his choice sale items.

"Hey, Ally – good gossip!" Rowan smiled, turning her attention to me.

"What?"

"Look!"

Rowan wafted what looked like a serviette under my nose.

"What does that say?" I squinted at a squiggle which was scrawled on the crushed paper. "'I.O.U. £10'. What's that for?"

"I showed the song to Chazza – and he really liked it!" Rowan squealed. "I won the bet!"

"Well, you won a serviette," I grinned. "When's he going to pay up properly?"

"Oh, sometime never," Rowan replied cheerfully. "He's never got any money, same as me. I'd have written him an I.O.U. too if I'd lost the bet. But anyway, that doesn't matter –"

My sister absentmindedly dabbed her nose with the paper napkin, then scrunched it up and shoved it in her pocket.

"– what matters is that Chazza's going to take the song to the rest of the band at the next rehearsal!"

"What song?" asked Tor.

"Just a *song* song," I replied vaguely, too excited

by what Rowan was saying to come up with anything more explicit. "Did you actually sing it for him, Ro?"

"Yeah, *right*!" she giggled. "We were in KFC!"

Well, that explained the squiggled-on serviette.

"I just tried to *hum* the tune to him," Rowan continued, "while he read the words. I'm going to his house tomorrow to sing it to him properly, when he's got his guitar with him and everything."

"That's brilliant," I felt myself beam. "But that's not gossip; that's just good news. So, spill the beans – what about Linn and Q?"

"Q?" repeated Tor, wrinkling his nose up just like he had at the kitchen table earlier.

Rowan narrowed her eyes and gave me a knowing little smile.

"Well," she began, "*apparently*, after me and you left on Friday night, Linn and Alfie went over to the bar –"

Oh, Alfie... My mind drifted off for a second, at the mere mention of his name.

"– and Q started flirting with Linn!"

"Yeah?" I gasped, getting back to the gossip at hand.

"*And* there's more. According to Chazza, she invited Q to the party she and Alfie were going to," Rowan announced, trying to settle herself down and wincing as a splinter tried to bite her bottom. (Honestly, Dad should put carpeting down in this place.)

"Did he go?" I asked.

"Oh, yes," said Rowan, very adamantly. "*And* she went out with him on Saturday night *and* last night!"

"Linn's got a *boy*friend!" Tor announced, putting his small finger on what was going on straight away.

"Maybe," nodded Rowan. "But –"

She playfully slapped her hands over Tor's ears to stop him hearing any more of our grown-up conversation.

"– Chazza says he's a total creep! This guy's really, really full of himself, *really* arrogant – the rest of the lads in the band can't stand him!"

"So," I frowned, as Tor giggled and wriggled his way out of Rowan's grasp, "what are they all doing being in a band with him, if they don't like him?"

"It's Q's band," Rowan explained. "He started it up."

"Q's a stupid name," Tor announced breathlessly, now that he'd escaped from Rowan's tickling clutches.

"Yeah – and Q might just be a stupid boy," Rowan muttered, shooting me a worried glance.

Linn could be a grouch sometimes, but she was *our* grouch.

What was she getting herself into? And did we dare ask her?*

(*Are you *kidding?*)

Chapter 10

DAD'S SECRET PAST, LINN'S SECRET PRESENT...

Wandering into the kitchen this Wednesday morning, my nose twitched to the intermingled breakfast smells of toast and pet food. (On separate plates and bowls, by the way – toast spread with Kit-e-Kat isn't one of Rowan's weird gastronomic experiments. Not *yet*, anyway.)

"Where's Dad?" I asked, pulling out a chair and gently persuading a cat that wasn't Colin to move off it so that I could sit down.

"He's run off to join the circus," muttered Linn, taking a sip of orange juice while she flicked through a magazine.

"He's gone for more milk – we've run out," said Rowan, more usefully.

She looked more like a Heidi than a Rowan today, with her two plaits pulled up and pinned across the top of her head. She should have been skipping across Swiss mountain tops in dirndl skirts instead of stomping off to Palace Gates School in her much-hated uniform.

"Mmm... I wonder *who* could have used up all the milk?" Linn asked pointedly, looking up from her magazine and narrowing her eyes at Tor, who seemed to be dunking his spoon in a bowl containing a few lonely Coco Pops floating on a lake of semi-skimmed.

"It's good for my bones!" Tor mumbled through a mouthful of milk.

"Well, *we* all have bones, too," Linn pointed out. "Just try and remember to leave a little bit of calcium in the carton for the rest of us next time, Tor."

She wasn't annoyed, not really. She never gets bugged by Tor or anything he does. She just saves up her annoyance for me and Rowan. Which is why neither of us was asking her anything about Q, or what was going on between them – although we were both gagging to find out.

"Look – I wanted to show Dad this," I said, holding up a blurred Polaroid for everyone's inspection.

"Is that *him*? Is that Dad?" asked Rowan, taking the photo from me for a closer inspection.

"Yep," I replied, pouring myself tea out of the pot.

I'd been lying in bed the night before, wondering how Rowan had got on singing her (our) song round at Chazza's house (instead of at KFC), when thoughts of bands and music had made me suddenly remember the fuzzy picture Ro was now poring over. Feeling decidedly non-sleepy, I'd thrown off my duvet, grabbed my box from the bottom of the wardrobe, and started rooting among the mounds of reject memorabilia I keep in there (all the nice, in-focus, thumb-free photos are in the official albums downstairs). And after a few minutes' happy rummaging, here was the snap I was looking for.

"God! He looks so young!" giggled Rowan.

"I know!" I smiled, then stopped smiling when I realized there was no milk for my tea.

"Here," said Linn, picking up Tor's bowl and pouring a splosh of milk into my mug before our brother had a chance to protest.

"Thanks," I mumbled, wishing there wasn't a couple of soggy Coco Pops drifting around in my drink – but then, I didn't want to come over all ungrateful.

"What's that big dark thing that Dad's holding?" asked Rowan, squinting at the hard-to-make-out Polaroid.

"Lemme see…" Tor insisted, slithering out of his chair and standing next to Ro for a better nosey. "Hey, it's a *dog*!"

"It's a *guitar*, Tor," I corrected him. "He must

have been mucking around with someone's guitar when that was taken."

Honestly, what's Tor like? He sees the world through animal-tinted glasses.

"No – that's *his* guitar," Linn surprised us by saying. "He was in a band for about five minutes when he first left school. Don't you remember him telling us?"

"*No*," I frowned, checking Rowan and Tor's faces for signs of confusion, so that I knew it wasn't just me, suffering from a case of long-term memory loss.

Yep, there was confusion. Phew – my brain cells *were* intact.

"Oh, yeah," shrugged Linn, obviously enjoying her position of eldest child: She Who Knows More Than the Rest of Us.

"Did they play gigs?" I asked, keen to find out more.

"No, they never played professionally," Linn shook her head. "They never even had a name. They only did a few rehearsals round each others' houses, and then it all fizzled out."

"So, Dad used to play guitar?" Rowan giggled. "Wow – I'd love to hear what *that* would sound like! I'll have to get Chazza to bring his round so Dad can have a go!"

"There's no need – he's still got that guitar," said Linn, pointing to the photo.

"Where?" I frowned, feeling sure I'd have noticed a guitar-shaped object lying around the house at *some* point over the last thirteen years that I'd lived here.

"Up in the attic storeroom," Linn replied, matter-of-factly. "It's funny, I was just talking to Q about it the other night, saying what a waste it was, sitting up there gathering dust in its case."

Linn stopped dead, realizing she'd accidentally introduced Q into the conversation. She didn't want to do *that* – not with her sisters in such close proximity (i.e. within potential teasing distance).

Me and Rowan shot quick glances at one another, wondering which one of us should jump in and take advantage of the situation with a carefully worded remark.

Only Tor got in there first.

"I don't like Q," he muttered, wrinkling his nose up in disgust.

"Tor! How can you not like him?" Linn frowned in surprise. "You haven't even *met* him!"

"He's a big, stupid show-off," Tor shrugged, swirling his milk-dribbling spoon in the air.

"*What*? Where are you getting this from, Tor? Ah … let me guess!"

Linn turned her gaze on Rowan. Oh, and what a scary, narrow-eyed gaze it was...

"Well, he *is* a big-head, Linnhe!" Rowan protested. "You can just tell that from watching him on stage! *And* I heard that he's been taking all the credit for writing Annihilator's songs, and he's only written *one* of them. *And* he thinks he's too good to muck in with the rest of the band and move all the gear on and off stage!"

"For *your* information, Rowan, Q is *not* a big-head!" said Linn, raising her voice. "Chazza's been saying all this stuff, hasn't he?"

Rowan said nothing, thinking that her staying stum would stop Chazza being implicated as the source of the gossip. As *if*.

"Well, I think Chazza's just jealous of Q being the frontman of the band," Linn announced, pushing her chair back and leaving the table. "And *you're* just jealous, Ro, 'cause *I'm* going out with Q and *you're* not!"

And with that, Linn stormed out of the kitchen, and – with a house-trembling slam – out of the front door.

Tor stared after her, while a cat that wasn't Colin spotted a window of opportunity and leapt on to the table to help itself to the bowl of Coco-Pop-flavoured milk.

"Guess that answers our question, then," I said to a stunned-looking Rowan. "I guess he *is* her boyfriend!"

"God – imagine Linnhe thinking I'm jealous!" Rowan huffed, dropping her chin on to her hands. "I was just trying to let her know what a creep Q is. Wish I hadn't bothered now!"

So did I. I had a funny feeling that the more Rowan had a downer on this guy, the more determined Linn would be to date him.

My sisters: they were truly talented at the graceful art of winding each other up...

Chapter 11

DOH! RAY, ME...

It was still Wednesday, it was about seven o'clock, and Grandma had just left to go home and settle down to an exciting night of soaps, chocolate digestives and knitting. Or maybe a night of sweet sherries with her main man. (For some reason, she's always very coy and cagey about her hot dates with Stanley.)

Dad had just left too, off out for an evening's worth of hooting, hollering and stomping along to "Achy, Breaky Heart", or whatever terrible country records they played at his line-dancing class.

Heidi – I mean, Rowan – was stretched out on the sofa, looking soulful and forlorn. In Rowan-speak, that meant she was still huffing and hurt after her little run-in with Linn over breakfast. She'd muttered something about having a sore throat, but I think she was suffering more from lightly bruised feelings.

Tor and I, meanwhile, were lounging on the beanbag, which wasn't as comfy as it sounds, since the beanbag was balanced on top of one of the armchairs (Tor's idea of an interesting experiment, which gives you some idea of how bored he was).

Linn was nowhere to be seen. She'd stomped in from school about five minutes after I got in, then stomped out, only stopping long enough to get changed, brush her already immaculate hair and tell Grandma she wouldn't be back for tea.

Grandma looked a bit put out – she doesn't approve of us not eating tea together (No. 36 on her infamous Disapproval List). She doesn't mind if we invite half of Crouch End to come and share it with us, as long as she can see my, Ro, Linn and Tor's faces somewhere in the crowd around the table. *And* she'd gone and done a new recipe tonight: ham cooked in Coca-Cola. (I know it sounds like one of Rowan's food-combining disasters, but it *was* a bona fide recipe from Grandma's telly chef heroine, Nigella Lawson.)

"That's the phone, Ally," murmured Rowan from her prone position, as the phone began to trill out in the hall.

"It sure is," I replied, keeping my eyes fixed on the TV. "And that's the dog."

Rolf hates the sound of the phone. Or maybe I've got that wrong – maybe he just gets a total thrill out of barking at it.

"Get the phone, Tor," Rowan pleaded, noticing that I wasn't about to budge.

"Can't – I'm stuck!" mumbled Tor, wriggling uselessly around beside me on the rustling beanbag like an upturned beetle.

"*Alleeeeee!*" Rowan whined pathetically. "My throat's sore!"

"OK, OK!" I sighed, pushing myself off the beanbag with a struggle and padding towards the hall, and the barking phone and ringing dog. Or whatever.

Rolf was delighted to see me, and to celebrate he decided to lick my bare feet. Don't ask me why – I hadn't smeared them in gravy or Pedigree Chum or anything.

"Hello? *Gerroff!*" I said distractedly down the phone, while trying to push Rolf and his soggy sandpaper tongue away from my tootsies.

"Huh?"

It was only a "huh"; the smallest of noises, but I recognized the owner of that "huh" straight away.

"I, uh … the dog. The 'gerroff' thing. I mean, I wasn't talking to you. Not that I don't want to. Um, I mean, Rolf – he was licking my … oh, never mind. Sorry. Uh, hello," I burbled pathetically.

"Oh, right," came Alfie's familiar, sweet-and-slow-as-syrup drawl. "Is Linn there?"

"Um, no. She's out. Out somewhere ... else," I burbled some more, flapping my hand uselessly in the air, like Alfie could *see* it.

Honestly, Alfie must think I suffer from *speech* dyslexia or something whenever he talks to me. It's like sentences leave my head fully formed, but then reach my mouth and jump out in a total psychotic jumble.

"Uh, any idea where?" he asked.

Actually, I didn't have any idea *where* Linn was, but after this morning, I had an idea who *with*.

"I, uh, dunno. Maybe you should, y'know, call her. On her mobile, I mean. Not here. Ha, ha, ha."

Shut up, shut up, shut up, I told myself off, while being vaguely aware of the doorbell ringing and Tor (freed from the quicksand beanbag) racing to answer it.

"Yeah, I tried that, but it's switched off," muttered Alfie. "Maybe she's out with Mary or Nadia."

"Or that guy Q..." I heard myself suggest.

"Mmm – well, maybe I *won't* bother trying to call her, then," Alfie replied, sounding ever so slightly – forgive me if I'm wrong – *bitter*.

What was this? Was Alfie jealous of Linn hanging out with another boy? Nah – it couldn't be that. He and Linn had been best mates for years, and there'd never been the merest *sniff* of romance between the pair of them (oh, foolish Linn!).

Or could it be that Alfie was as unimpressed with Linn's choice of boyfriend as Rowan and I were? Was he another recruit for the Q Non-Fan Club?

"Erm ... well, I'll tell her you called," I blustered, my mind whirling with questions for Alfie, along the lines of "Do you have a problem with Q?" and "Could you ever see yourself being madly, wildly attracted to me?" Neither of which I actually came out with, of course, thanks to my Alfie-related speech dyslexia.

"Whatever," he mumbled in a flat voice. "See you, Ally."

"See you, Alfie," I replied softly, even though the phone had already gone dead.

He *definitely* didn't like Q. I was absolutely sure of it; specially with that last, gloomy-sounding "whatever". How weird...

"Ally! Look, Chazza's here!" Rowan twittered, as soon as I stepped back into the living room.

Gee, thanks for telling me, Ro – I'd never have noticed... I thought to myself, giving Chazza a quick nod hello and getting the merest hint of a nod in return. Or maybe he'd just developed a twitch.

"He's just on his way to rehearsals," Rowan began to explain, "and he came by to run through the song I wrote, before he plays it for the other lads tonight."

Oops – looked like I'd given Alfie false information. If the band were rehearsing tonight, Linn *couldn't* be out with Q and his unfeasibly big head.

Just as that thought was rumbling through my mind, I noticed that both Chazza and Rowan were staring at me. It was kind of unnerving. Chazza – like Von – never usually acknowledges my existence. (Nothing personal, you understand – I'm just a lesser-spotted younger sister, i.e. of very little interest.)

And now Tor, Rolf and a newly arrived Winslet were all staring at me too, since it seemed the fashionable thing to do. What was wrong? Had I grown another nose while I'd been on the phone or something?

"Chazza just wants to make sure he's got the tune right," Rowan broke the silence. "So I told him you'd sing it for him."

"Yeah, *right*!" I snorted, feeling a well of panic rising in my chest. What was Rowan playing at?

"Go on, Al!" Rowan pleaded with me. "I can't sing with my bad throat, and ... and I told Chazza that you knew all the words because you listened all the time when I was writing it!"

Rowan had her big "I'm-spinning-a-line-but-please-go-along-with-it!" look on her face. So she'd managed to keep up the whole story that she wrote the song all by herself.

"Nah!" I shook my head and went to walk out.

"Please, Ally!"

That was Chazza. He'd *actually* communicated with me. He wanted to hear me sing. *Me* – little, inconsequential, usually invisible Ally Love.

OK, I'm shallow; I was so flattered by those two grunted words of Chazza's that I found myself shrugging and more or less agreeing – in that one small movement – to sing.

"Great!" Rowan enthused, looking a lot perkier now than she had when I left her moping on the sofa a few minutes before. "Go for it, Ally!"

What could I do?

Well, what I *could* do was close my eyes, so I couldn't see the five sets of expectant eyes fixed on me (three pairs human, two pairs canine). What I could *also* do to make it easier was imagine the song was about me and Alfie instead of Billy and Anita, who'd inspired it.

I took a deep breath, blanked out the world (or at least the living room and the people and dogs in it) and began.

"*You smile* – erk!" I croaked, then coughed.

Mmm, nice start.

Try again...

"*You smile, but it makes me shiver,*
You look my way and it makes me shake,
Every time you talk to me
I'm sure it's just some mistake.
There's no point to loving you,
There's no point in all this pain,
There's no way this is going to happen,
Why put myself through it again and again?"

I stopped, and the only sound in the room seemed to be my heart thumping. Not in time, by the way.

"Is that enough?" I asked, daring to open one eye, now I'd warbled my way through the first verse.

"Do the chorus," said Chazza, who'd unzipped the soft case from around his guitar while I'd had my eyes tight shut.

"OK," I replied, shutting both eyes closed again.

There was a soft strum of the guitar, which threw me off a bit. Then I recognized the tune Chazza was playing, and began to sing the next bit of the song.

"People say love is special,
But I think love is tough,
'Cause I know you like me,
Just not enough,
Not enough,
Not enough…"

My overworked heart pitter-pattered (or thunkety-thunked, more like) when I heard Chazza's deep, growly voice join in with mine for the last couple of lines.

OK – that was all I could do. I was hyperventilating so much that I'd have passed out if I'd attempted the next verse.

I dared to open my eyes, and got ready for the stick I was about to take. Only there wasn't any.

"Brilliant!" said Ro enthusiastically, while Tor clapped manically.

This was all right. I'd sung, and no one had barfed. In fact, it was better than that – no one had howled. Or should I say, no *dog* had howled.

Move over, Madonna-*awwwwhooooooooo*!

Chapter 12

SEVEN COKES, ONE ORANGINA AND A LEER, PLEASE...

"*Whiiiiiit-whoooooooooooooooo!*"

Don't panic – that wasn't me singing again.

(Phew! sighs a relieved world.)

It was Chloe wolf-whistling at Billy. Or, more precisely, it was Chloe wolf-whistling at Billy's bum as he bent over to chuck his bowling ball down the aisle (or alley, or lane, or whatever its technical name is).

"Oi!" Kyra chipped in, as she slipped a scrunchie off her wrist and tangled her bouncing curls into a top-knot. "We can see your knickers, Billy Stevenson! Are they Calvins, or did your mum buy them for you from BHS?!"

Poor Billy – I'd dragged him to the Finsbury Park ten-pin bowling alley this Friday night 'cause I thought he was in serious need of cheering up; but all this heckling from my so-called friends was only going to make him paranoid as *well* as glum.

Yep, it had been over a week since Billy had told me about his Big Dump (I mean the *love* kind of dump, of *course*), but he was still pathetically pining for the cruel, heartless Anita. So, I'd thought that going out with seven gorgeous girlies just *might* help massage his dented ego. Only I couldn't find him seven gorgeous girlies, so he'd had to make do with me and my motley mates. (Fnar.)

My mates – who were under *strict* instructions to be extra nice to Billy. Not that they'd taken the slightest notice of what *I* said. They seemed to have interpreted the words "Billy's had a rough time lately, so be sweet", as "Please feel free to tease Billy senseless at every opportunity".

"Do you need a hand with that?" Salma shouted over to Billy, as he frantically shoved the top of his cotton boxer shorts down under the waistband of his skate shorts.

She turned and winked at us lot, just as Billy's fumbling made him lose control of his bowling ball and drop it with a resounding *thwack!* on the polished pine floor. Even above the pounding R'n'B music that was thundering out of the PA, nearly everyone in the place heard that ominous *thwack!* and turned to stare in our direction.

Course, Jen and Kellie weren't helping by cracking up laughing like a couple of hysterical hyenas. Having Billy there as the butt of everyone's joke was the best Friday night's entertainment they'd had in ages.

"Poor Billy..." I muttered out loud, peering at my (boy) friend through the splayed fingers with which I'd covered my face.

He was sprinting after the runaway ball now – which was ambling off down the lane towards the pins – with one hand still self-consciously stuffing bits of boxer short back in place. Now absolutely *everyone* was staring in our direction; at this rate we were bound to get chucked out soon for causing a disturbance. Or at least be presented with a bill for the moon-size crater Billy had made in the floor...

"But you know something, Ally?" whispered Sandie, who was sitting right next to me. "I think Billy's kind of enjoying all the fuss."

"Nah!" I shook my head, putting myself in his position. If it was *me* out with Billy and *his* posse of mates, and they were all bellowing at me about my pants, I think I'd have pretended to go to the loo and jumped on the nearest bus home long ago.

"Hey – whose turn is it to go up to the bar?" Chloe suddenly asked, turning round and tinkling the ice cubes around in her empty glass of Coke.

"I'll go," I offered, since it was a good excuse not to watch the girls psychologically *maul* my mate to embarrassed shreds.

"I'll give you a hand," said Sandie, standing up and grabbing a fistful of coins from the kitty on the plastic table beside us.

Exactly ten seconds later, we were joined by another pair of helping hands in the unexpected shape of Kyra.

"Hi!" she grinned, sliding on to a plastic stool beside me and Sandie.

"What's wrong?" I grinned back at her. "Got bored of teasing Billy? Maybe you should ask around, see if there's any bear-baiting going on in the neighbourhood tonight. That'd be fun!"

"Ha ha!" Kyra smirked sarcastically, as she twirled an escaped curl in her fingers. "Anyway, who are you kidding? You can't tell me Billy isn't *loving* it!"

"See?" said Sandie, niggling me a little by siding with Kyra.

Honestly, who knew Billy the best out of the three of us? *Me*, actually, if my girl friends hadn't noticed.

"So, this guy that your sister's going out with – how cute is he?" drawled Kyra, sliding her elbows on to the bar top and switching the conversation to her favourite subject (boys) with the greatest of ease. "You know, on a scale of one to ten. Like, compared to that cute guy serving drinks…"

Both Sandie and I stared down the bar at the

undeniably cute lad who was currently hunting in the refrigerated units for the Orangina Jen had asked us to get her.

Aha – so *that*'s why Kyra had so kindly offered her services ... to get a closer gawp at the young bartender.

"He must be at least eighteen!" Sandie whispered at Kyra, sounding slightly shocked.

"So? There's no harm in just *looking*," shrugged Kyra.

"*Leering*, you mean," I pointed out, deliberately leaning my head right over when I spoke so that I blocked her scenic view.

"Who cares what you call it?" Kyra widened her eyes saucily at me. "Take a look – he's a definite nine out of ten."

"I guess so," I muttered, now a bit distracted by the certified cuteness of Orangina-hunting barman. "Well, that guy Q that Linn's seeing: he'd definitely be a nine out of ten, too, if he didn't fancy himself so much."

"But how come you and Rowan have such a downer on him?" asked Kyra.

See, the trouble with Kyra is that she thinks prettiness is a redeeming factor. A lad could be a serial nose-picker with all the charm of sludge, but if he was halfway good-looking, Kyra would *still* fancy him. (Hey – remember she *did* date Richie/Ricardo for ages, and a snail in a coma has more personality in its little antennae than Richie/Ricardo.)

"I told you – Q's a big-head!" I tried to explain. "He was a big-head when I saw him on stage last week—"

"God, I wish I could have been there!" Kyra interrupted with a sigh.

And that's the other trouble with Kyra – the tiniest, weeniest whiff of celebrity and she comes over all star-struck. You know how she chased that band we saw at the MTV studios in Camden? Well, she got their autograph, but didn't recognize any of the names they'd scribbled down. And yet she was *still* chuffed. Which is why she was now beginning to turn her star-struck gaze in the direction of Chazza's band, even though I knew she'd hate the stuff they played. There's about as much chance of Kyra liking noisy, gloomy, indie rock music as there is of me dating Alfie. And I think we *all* know the chances of that happening. (Clue: never.)

"Well, here's a good example of why Q's a total big-head," I began again, struggling to get my point across. "On Wednesday night, the band were rehearsing, right? And he only goes and turns up with my *sister*."

Oh, yes, I hadn't been telling Alfie fiberoonies the other night – Linn and Q *were* out together.

"So?" said Kyra, doing that annoying lip-curl thing she sometimes does that makes you feel about *that* interesting.

"Wait! I hadn't finished!" I defended myself, dying to tell Kyra and Sandie the gossip Rowan had whispered to me after tea tonight. "The thing was, the lads had all agreed that there'd be absolutely no girlfriends at rehearsals, but Q brings Linn along all the same. Then he does this whole posing show for Linn while he sings the songs, winking and wiggling his hips at her like he's a teenage Tom Jones or something."

"Yeuch!" squeaked Sandie, wrinkling up her nose.

"Cool!" sighed Kyra dreamily.

"It's not cool – he's a total slimeball!" I insisted. "*And* he's a slimeball who'll be in my house right now!"

"How come?" asked Sandie. "What's he doing at your house tonight?"

"He and Linn are babysitting Tor," I winced.

Oh, yes: while the rest of the family were having fun somewhere or other (Dad had been invited out beer-drinking with line-dancing chums; Rowan was off somewhere seedily glamorous with Von and

Chazza; Grandma had joined a Learn-to-Speak-Spanish class with Stanley; I was at the ten-pin bowling alley despairing at Kyra), poor, innocent Tor was having to suffer the lovey-doveyness of Linn and the less than lovely Q.

"Oooh!" cooed Kyra. "We should all go back to your place after this and check him out!"

"Yeah? What happened to staying here and checking out that cute barman?" I grinned at her.

My grin soon vanished as Sandie elbowed me sharply in the ribs at the same time as I heard a cough.

"Ahem. Anything else?" said the cute barman, clattering a tray piled with Cokes (not forgetting the Orangina) in front of me.

"Yes," I nodded. "A large hole in the ground please, for me to disappear into and *die*."

OK, so I didn't say anything quite that witty and smart.

What I *actually* said, was "Nuh-unghh" (or something like it), before I grabbed the tray, spilt half the Coke on to the tray 'cause I was shaking so much, and left Sandie to pay up.

But I'm sure the cute guy was still pretty impressed by me.

Like, *right*...

* * *

It was exactly 12.30 a.m. according to the luminous read-out on my digital bedside clock – which meant it was actually 12.17 a.m., since I'd set the clock wrong when I first got it and never got around to fixing it. (Hey, I'd only had the thing three years – give me a break!)

Anyhow, at exactly 12.17 a.m., there I was in my nearly pitch-black bedroom, with only the snoring of something furry somewhere to keep me company, with three thoughts trundling around in my sleep-free mind.

And those were…

1) No matter what I do, I am always destined to act like a complete dork in front of cool older boys. And that's a sad but true fact.

2) I know *nothing*. There I was, feeling sorry for Billy tonight, when all the time, Sandie and Kyra were right – he *was* loving it. On the way back to the table with my sloshing tray of Cokes, Billy somehow (miraculously) got a strike, and although he might have been as pinkly pink as a very shy prawn, he did look decidedly thrilled to have four squealing girlies (Chloe, Salma, Jen and Kellie) hurl themselves bodily at him as if he was the David Beckham of ten-pin bowling. Oh, well, at least he cheered up.

3) Was Kyra right about something else? *Was* it

weird that I had such a downer on Q, when the only time I'd ever seen him was the night of the gig? OK, so he acted like a real show-off plonker then, and Rowan *had* heard a bunch of bad stories about him, but he wasn't exactly Jack the Ripper or anything.

And the two reasons I was lying awake at 12.17 a.m. (sorry, 12.18 a.m. now) thinking kindlier thoughts about Q were...

1) He made Linn really happy. I mean *really* happy. When I'd rolled in from bowling, he'd only just left, and Linn was practically *levitating* about the house with happiness. And trust me – it's not very often you see our Linn in a state of tran- scendental bliss (i.e. smiling). If Q could make such a difference to the Queen of Grouch, then maybe, just maybe, he was ... all right.

2) I'd suddenly remembered that I didn't like Kyra much (i.e. not at all) when I first met her, and now the irritating-but-fun old moo was one of my best mates – so maybe Q deserved a chance too. Perhaps Linn would introduce us sometime and I'd see a kind, funny, sweet side to him that's totally different to the persona he'd put on as the frontman in the band. Perhaps he'd be really sensitive, and stop and talk to me, instead of just mumbling a brief "hello" in my direction, like Chazza and Alfie (sigh!) usually did. Perhaps—

"Ally?" said a small voice, accompanied by a small, dark shadow slipping into my room.

"Nightmare?" I asked, tossing back the duvet cover to make space for my little brother.

(The something that had been contentedly snoring let out an indignant *prrrp!* as it got smothered in duvet.)

"That's Derek," muttered a shadowy Tor, recognizing a cat that wasn't Colin and hauling it out of danger and into bed with us.

"Did you have a nightmare, babes?" I repeated, feeling Tor's cold feet warm themselves on my goose-pimpling legs.

"No."

"Couldn't you sleep?"

"No."

"Why not?"

I felt Tor shrug beside me.

Right: I needed to wheedle the information out of the Boy of Very Little Words in a different way. I'd start by chatting about something else entirely.

"Did you have a nice time tonight with Linn and Q?"

"No."

Uh-oh.

"Why not?" I asked, frowning in the dark.

"He snogged Linn on the sofa when I was trying to watch *101 Dalmatians*."

"Yuck," I shuddered, more to make Tor laugh than anything. I was still determined to stop having a downer on Q – and failure to watch and enjoy a Disney movie didn't make Linn's boyfriend a bad guy in my book (even if it scored nil points in Tor's).

"And he said all cats had fleas."

Ah … just a silly, offhand, jokey remark.

"And that Rolf had stinky breath."

True – but maybe a bit rude, even if Rolf didn't understand that he was being slagged off.

"And I told him about rescuing Britney, and *he* said that pigeons were rats with wings and they had *germs*."

OK – that was definitely showing a lack of sensitivity.

"And he pointed at Mum's painting and sniggered."

"Did he realize that Mum had painted it?" I quizzed Tor.

"Uh-huh. Linn told him. And he still sniggered. He sniggered at all our stuff."

I'd heard enough. Somehow, the idea of this guy trawling around our house was practically as creepy as those burglars rummaging around the place, sneering at all our much-loved knick-knacks.

Instantly, I took back all the positive thoughts I was trying to muster about Q and chucked them in my mental waste bin.

"What did Linn say to all this?" I asked, aghast.

"She didn't say anything – she just giggled."

This ... this was worse than I thought.

It wasn't just stupid stuff like taking offence about fleas and rats with wings; it was about Linn not standing up for anyone in the family – from Tor through to Rolf through to Mum.

Falling for this guy seemed to be messing with my sister's head, and that was kind of *scary*...

Chapter 13

HELP THE HAMSTERS!

"Say yes!"

"No."

"Yes!"

"No! I told you, Kyra, I am *not* asking Rowan to sneak us both in to the gig next week. No way!"

"Why not?" pleaded Kyra.

"'Cause they're playing at the Student Union," I told her for the tenth time. "Big fancy colleges aren't exactly easy to sneak into!"

"Course they are!" insisted Kyra, not taking no for an answer.

"Look – I just don't want to, OK?"

A couple of weeks ago at school, we did this Social Studies thing, looking at the hardships and sheer terror endured by asylum seekers fleeing across dangerous borders and terrains. Me – I'm such a wuss, I could never deal with something like that. Being smuggled into a pub under age had practically given me a heart attack and I wasn't in a hurry to go through *that* stress again.

"Aw, Ally, come on!" Kyra wheedled. "That's not fair – you just want to keep the band to yourself!"

That was a joke. For a start, Annihilator had been rubbish when I saw them. And secondly, there was no way I wanted to watch that guy Q and his big head (and small talent) prance around a stage again.

Nope, the only *possible* reason I'd want to see them play was...

"What about that song you and Rowan wrote?" asked Kyra, putting her finger right on it. "Don't you want to hear it being performed for the very first time?"

"I'm not that bothered," I lied with a shrug.

"You're kidding!" Kyra frowned at me, looking disappointed that her emotional blackmail didn't seem to be working.

"Whatever," I shrugged again, hoping she wasn't going to push the point.

Of *course* I was gagging to hear my song played by the band. Even if super-creep Q was singing it. But I'd rather just be patient and wait to hear it on tape sometime.

Kyra sighed long and loud, and turned her attention back to the CD track-listing she'd been studying before she'd started her "*please* can we go to the gig, *please* can we go to the gig" rant.

"So what does your song go like?" she asked, distractedly.

"I showed you the words already," I pointed out to her.

I'd let Kyra and Sandie take a look at my scribbled lyrics one day at break last week. Sandie couldn't stop saying how good they were (aw, shucks!), so I knew she was pretty impressed. Kyra didn't say anything – so I knew she was pretty impressed, too.

"I didn't mean the words," said Kyra, sticking the CD back in the rack. "I meant the *tune*."

"Um…" I mused, trying to figure out what to compare it to. "I guess it's a bit like that old 'Creep' song by Radiohead."

"But I don't know that one," Kyra wrinkled her nose at me. "Go and sing it!"

"What, 'Creep'?"

"No, silly – *your* song."

"No way!" I grinned.

"Go on!" Kyra urged me.

"No!"

"Yes!"

"No!"

"God, Ally," Kyra sighed theatrically. "Why not?"

"'Cause we're in Woolies!" I hissed at her.

"So?" shrugged Kyra, glancing around her at the Saturday-afternoon crowds as if they mattered not one tiny bit.

Well, Kyra might be 100 per cent fearless, but I wasn't about to be sued by Woolworth's for frightening away their customers with my warblings.

"Anyway, I've got to go," I said, suddenly noticing the time. "It's my turn to make tea tonight."

"Hmm..." murmured Kyra, disinterestedly. "Hey, Ally, before you go –"

"What?" I asked.

Kyra bit her lip and looked pleadingly at me.

"Can we go to the gig next week?" she simpered. "Please? Pretty please? Pretty please with sugar on top?"

"Kyra! Listen to me: N. O. spells—"

"Yes!" she interrupted, clapping her hands together excitedly. "God, Ally, we'll have *such* a brilliant time!"

That Kyra Davies – she must have got her Girl Guide badge in Perseverance...

"Do you want to buy a badge?" asked Tor's buddy Freddie, holding one under my nose for my inspection. "We've got lots!"

After Kyra making my head go twisty this afternoon, it was a bit of light relief to bumble home and see how the Hamster Rescue Association sale was going, back at our house. Or back at our garden gate, to be precise. Tor had set up a battered old picnic table on the pavement, piled it high with rubbish, and spent a happy afternoon guilt-tripping passing neighbours into parting with cash for junk.

"Ooh, I didn't know you'd got these made up, guys!" I commented, staring at the "Help the Hamsters!" slogan running rainbow-shaped over the top of an image of a small furry creature. With fangs.

It was a pity, really, that Tor had decided to use a picture of Mad Max for the badges, instead of one of the undoubtedly cuter furballs rescued by the Hamster Rescue Association. Max had a lot of character, all right, but he certainly didn't look like a hamster in need of help. He looked more like he needed a leash, or a *muzzle*, maybe. No wonder the boys had plenty of them left...

"Yep, we've got badges, an' ... an' ... an' *stuff*," said Freddie, the expert salesman, as he swept an arm over the skant array of *bits* that was left on the table.

"Mmmm, let me see ... what will I have?" I muttered, stalling for time as I perused the packet of out-of-date Hula Hoops, a tube of only slightly squeezed toothpaste and lightly (dog-)chewed Chewbacca figurine among the choice tat.

Tor and Freddie frowned in concentration after I made a grab at a few things and asked them how much I owed them.

"Um ... 36p?" Freddie guessed wildly, looking to Tor for his approval. Tor nodded sagely.

"Tell you what, boys – here's £1, since it's for a good cause!" I grinned, dropping the cash into their margarine-tub till before I headed off into the house with an armful of stuff that I seemed to remember donating in the first place.

Only I didn't quite get round to leaving. Not when I heard Linn approaching, making a very unexpected noise – i.e. *giggling*.

"Oh, hi, Ally!" she beamed, holding her handbag with one hand and – urgh – Q with the other.

"Hi..." I mumbled, casting my eyes at close quarters over the smirking lad that was attached to my sister.

He was wearing these baggy trousers that were only *just* hanging on to his hips, so you got a little flash of muscly tummy where his un-ironed Diesel T-shirt didn't quite cover him up. I guess you could say he was pretty in a slightly grungy, Damon-Albarn-out-of-Blur way, but I wasn't Kyra – or Linn. I wasn't about to go all giggly and girlie and be impressed by him and his indie boy-band looks.

"Q turned up out of the blue and met me from work tonight – didn't you?" Linn gushed, in a very un-Linn kind of way.

Q didn't say anything, just smirked a smirk and ran his hand through his short-ish, scruffy-ish hair.

"I'm just going to get changed and then we're going out," Linn trilled at me. "So don't make anything for my tea, OK?"

"Mmm," I mumbled non-committally.

"Heh, heh, heh! What's this supposed to be?" Q sniggered, pointing at the sign that was Sellotaped to the edge of the picnic table.

"Do you like it?" Freddie beamed, pointing at Rowan's handmade "Hamster Rescue Association" sequinned extravaganza, unaware that Q was the enemy.

"Who made it?" Q guffawed. "Is it a Care in the Community project?"

I stopped breathing for a second – totally stunned.

Freddie looked confused, but Tor was frowning. He didn't know exactly what Q meant, but Detective Tor was smart enough to work out that it was a definite slag of some sort.

I looked at Linn, waiting for her to tell him off for belittling our sister and disabled people and Tor's good intentions all in one untactful swoop ... but she didn't.

"Oh, *you*!" she giggled again, pulling him by the hand up the garden path and into our house.

As they walked off, Tor stared silently up at me and made a face like he'd just stepped in dog poo.

"*Exactly*," I nodded down at him in total agreement...

Chapter 14

OH, WHAT A PERFECT DAY (ISH)

There was a Very Tiny Thing hopping about in the darkness. It was quite a sweet Very Tiny Thing, but it was pretty hard to work out what it *was* exactly.

"*I* think it's ... um ... a bit like a sparrow. But with fur. On stilts," came Alfie's voice, very, very close beside me.

I could hear him, but not see him; the Twilight World at London Zoo is a light-free zone thanks to its hoppity nocturnal inhabitants.

"Crossed with a bush baby?" I suggested, squinting at the Very Tiny Thing's rounder-than-round eyes, and managing – miraculously – not to stammer, stutter or speak gibberish for an entire sentence.

(OK – it was just five words, but it was a bit of an achievement for me, in the presence of the Mighty Alfie.)

"Yeah ... but what about that long wiggly snout it's got?" murmured my No. 1 love god, who was obviously deeply in awe of the Very Tiny Thing bounding around between artfully positioned twigs on the other side of the glass from us.

"It's a small-eared elephant shrew!" Tor whispered, setting us straight, as he breathed a contented fuzzy circle of condensation on to the glass.

"Is this your favourite thing in the zoo today?" I asked Tor, absorbing the radiating beams of sheer joy emanating from my kid brother.

"Maybe," he sighed happily. "What have you liked best, Ally?"

"The ring-tailed lemur," I told him. (I tell him that *every* time we come to the zoo, but he always asks anyway.)

"What have *you* liked best, Alfie?" Tor's voice enquired through the darkness.

"Uh … when Ally got to hold that tarantula," came Alfie's reply. "That was *really* cool."

Wow – me, Alfie and Tor spending a fun Sunday together; me managing to speak and act almost like a real human in front of Alfie; me actually *impressing* Alfie (thanks to my Crocodile Dundee deadly-spider-handling skills).

Oh, what a perfect day...

And then I woke up.

Well, that's what you expected me to say, wasn't it? BUT – pinch me hard 'cause I can't quite believe it – it was all *true*! (Except the part about the deadly-spider handling; I only got to *stroke* the thing when the zookeeper girl was doing a talk in the Reptile House earlier.)

So, how come?

Not how come I stroked a tarantula, I mean. More like, how come I was having such a perfect day, with my perfectly cute kid brother, and my perfectly perfect dream boy? Let me explain...

FIRST! Linn had promised Tor all week that she'd take him to the zoo, but he wasn't exactly *thrilled* to the core of his being when she announced over breakfast today that – argh! – she'd invited Q to come too. Specially not since Q had scoffed so openly at Tor's sterling fund-raising efforts only the day before.

SECOND! Not looking forward to playing Tor-in-the-middle, my quick-thinking brother *begged* me to keep him company – very loudly and in front of Dad (meaning that Linn had to grin and bear the idea of me busting up her cutesy plan of playing the caring big sister while snogging the face off her boyfriend).

THIRD! While Linn was preening in front of the bathroom mirror, making herself gorgeous for Creepy Q, the phone had rung. I answered – hoping it might be Q saying that he'd suddenly remembered he had to emigrate to Australia and couldn't make the zoo *after* all – and found myself voice to voice with Alfie. I think it's safe to say that Alfie sounded v., v., *v.* hacked off when I told him what the day's plans were. It turned out that a week or so ago, before love had completely fried her brain, Linn had half-invited *Alfie* along on the zoo outing, if he'd nothing else on. "Well, er … why don't you come anyway?" I heard myself ask him. I was still in shock at my downright shameless cheek, when I heard Alfie say, "Uh… OK! I will!"

And he did. And that's the story behind my perfect day. Only certain things about it made it less than perfect, just perfect-*ish*…

"Look at the time," muttered Alfie, a round dot of neon watch-face lighting up our little patch of Twilight World. "It's three o'clock already – we agreed to meet Linn and … *whatsisname* back at the café."

Boo.

See what I mean about the day being only perfect-*ish*? Did we *have* to spoil a beautiful thang and hook up with that boring twosome, who'd preferred to go off and *drool* at each other instead of cooing over furry long-nosed sparrows on stilts with us?

"Come on, Tor; time to say bye to the shrew!" I

said, reaching for my brother's hand before I led him through the shadowy throng of tourists huddled around the other glass cages, all tapping at the cute animals through the glass, just above the illuminated signs that read "PLEASE DON'T TAP ON THE GLASS".

The hand I grabbed was warm and … and too big to be Tor-sized.

"Oh, sorry!" I squeaked, letting go of Alfie's hand as fast as if I'd been *zapped* by 5000 volts.

"Uh … no problem," Alfie replied, sounding suspiciously like he was grinning.

Thank you, thank you, *thank* you, Twilight World, for being so pitch-black that no one could see my fiery-red face – except, of course, all the see-in-the-dark nocturnal hoppity things…

Y'know, any passing zoologist would have had a field day studying the prehistoric animal behaviour going on around the plastic picnic table this Sunday afternoon.

At first I couldn't think what Alfie and Q reminded me of, and then it hit me. Months ago, Tor had made all of us watch this really snooze-ville documentary about deer in the Scottish mountains. I don't remember much about it – 'cause I was too busy counting my *nose*, or daydreaming about watching *paint* dry, I was so bored – but one thing that did stick in my mind was a scene where two stags kept circling this female deer, pretending to ignore each other but really squaring up for a full-on, horn-clunking punch-up.

"So, have you had a nice day?" Linn smiled at Tor, when we'd all met up in the café forecourt.

Sitting to one side of Linn was Q, gazing off into the distance, a pair of RayBans perched on his snooty face, even though the sun was staying resolutely behind the clouds. On the other side of her, Alfie stared off into a *different* distance, trying to look casual, even though he was clenching his jaws so tight I could practically hear his teeth grind.

"Tor?" Linn repeated.

Then I noticed that another male in our party was doing the staring-off-into-the-distance silent-treatment thing.

Good *grief*. Tor had reverted to his most wordless mode, presumably to show Linn how irked he was by her paying more attention to Q than to us and the assorted animals on show. And presumably Q was being silent just to demonstrate his disinterest and sheer coolness to the rest of us – specially Alfie.

Alfie, meanwhile, was staying stum to indicate his disapproval of Q. And Linn ... Linn was giving *me* the silent treatment, for a) coming along today in the first place; and b) inviting Alfie. (I guess there's nothing like having a not-so-little sister and a best buddy tagging along to burst a romantic bubble...)

And me? Well, now that I'd found myself yanked out of the dark, comforting atmosphere of the Twilight World, and plunged into the tense, spotlight-bright atmosphere out here, I'd (pathetically) lost all my confidence and didn't dare open my mouth in front of Alfie again in case a bunch of complete wiffle fell out.

(It might have had something to do with the fact that I was still reeling from the accidental hand-holding thing, of course...)

"*Tor?*" said Linn, a little more loudly, a little more perplexed at Tor's behaviour.

"He's fine," Alfie suddenly chipped in, sounding slightly irritated. "We had a good time, didn't we, Tor? We saw the—"

"Hey, Linn," Q interrupted, swivelling his shades in my sister's direction. "Fancy going into the West End after this? Just me and you?"

"Oh, yeah! That would be great!" Linn grinned in surprise at Q, totally oblivious to the fact that her closest friend – the lovely, laid-back Alfie – looked just about ready to *explode*. "You guys will be all right taking Tor home, won't you?"

"Um, s'pose so..." I mumbled, since Alfie seemed to be struggling for something to say that didn't involve a swear word or three.

"Great," Linn smiled, before she got distracted by Q leaning over and wrapping his arm around her, like a python curling itself around a blissfully ignorant white mouse. (Hey, maybe I'd been hanging around the zoo too long...)

And so, ten minutes later, I found myself perched next to Tor on the top deck of a jiggling, rumbling bus home, staring at the scruffy, spiky, blondy hair of the boy sitting directly in front of us, and wondering what exactly was whirring about in Alfie's head right now.

I soon found out.

"Going to go sit at the front!" Tor announced, as he spotted someone getting up and made a dive for his favourite spot on the bus.

"Y'know ... I'm not jealous of that guy Q or anything," Alfie suddenly announced, swinging around in his seat and launching into a conversation with me now that Tor was out of earshot.

(*Do you hear yourself, Ally? This is a* conversation. *You will be expected to* reply. *Don't blow it!*)

"I know," I shrugged.

(*There, that wasn't so bad, was it?*)

"It's just that I've heard ... stuff about him," Alfie mumbled vaguely, running a hand through his hair.

He was so close, it was all I could do to resist reaching over and touching the thin leather band he wears tied round his wrist.

"Stuff?" I asked, keeping my side of the conversation to manageable, bite-sized chunks.

"Yeah – I've heard he's a total prat. Fancies himself, y'know?"

I knew.

"Rowan's heard that too."

"Yeah?"

"Yeah," I nodded.

(*Look – no stammering or bumbling! Maybe I've cracked it; maybe the way to hold it together in front of Alfie is to talk to him in sentences of five words or less!*)

"I've tried telling Linn he's a prat, but she just won't listen," Alfie shrugged sadly.

"Same with Rowan."

"Yeah?"

"Yeah."

Ooh, this was much better than the Twilight World – this way I got to look straight into his weirdly pale grey eyes...

And that was it: that was the end of our conversation. But it was OK – for the rest of the bus ride home, we sat in companionable silence, with Alfie still half-facing me, leaning along the back of the seat as he gazed soulfully out of the window.

It was better than OK – it was close to perfect. It was downright perfect-*ish*.

Chapter 15

GUESS WHO'S COMING TO DINNER?

"What do you think 'Q' stands for?" I mused, as I watched Rowan painting delicate daisy petals on top of the lilac varnish she'd just applied to my toenails.

"Quite Horrible?" she suggested, her head bent over my foot in concentration.

It was Thursday evening, it was just before tea, and we were both meant to be doing our homework. Only somehow I'd ended up sitting on my sister's bed, allowing myself to be a nail-art guinea pig. (Though Rowan had experimented on herself first; her own toenails were painted blue, with miniature yellow sunflowers dotted on them.)

It had been a hard week as far as concentration went; every time I tried to turn my head to thoughts of anything remotely worthwhile and sensible, my mind just skipped right off and started daydreaming about Alfie and our new common bond (i.e. disliking Q).

Funny, the things that can bring people

together… (OK, so we weren't together *together*, but don't start getting pernickety.)

"No, but really; what *does* 'Q' stand for?" I asked again. "I mean, the guys in the band are at college with him – don't they know his real name? The lecturers don't call him Q, do they?"

"Don't know…" Rowan murmured. "I'll ask Chazza. Hey, did I tell you that they're definitely going to be playing 'Not Enough…' at the gig on Saturday?"

"No. I mean, you didn't say they were *definitely* playing it – only that they *might*," I replied, suddenly remembering that I had a problem. All week, Kyra had still been adamant that we were going to go to this gig at the Student Union, and I was just as adamant that we weren't. But I might as well have been speaking ancient Greek to Kyra, for all the notice she'd taken of me telling her that it wasn't going to happen.

"Listen, you don't *mind* if we stick to the secret, do you?" Rowan suddenly blinked apologetically, holding a dribbling nail-varnish brush aloft. "About me writing it on my own, I mean?"

"Course I don't," I shrugged.

Course I did – my chest was just about *exploding* with pride at the idea of the band doing a song that little old me co-wrote. But I knew as well as my sister that if Chazza & Co ever found out that a thirteen-year-old girl had had a hand in writing it, "Not Enough..." would seem about as cool as doing a cover of a nursery rhyme. (Not fair, but true.)

"Oh, good – I was really hoping that didn't bug you, 'cause I'm *so* excited about the idea of hearing our song played live. That's *if* Annihilator are still together by the weekend, of course," Rowan muttered, before lifting her work of art (my tootsies) and blowing the nail polish dry (it tickled).

"What are you on about?" I frowned at her.

"I *mean*, Q the Quite Horrible has been driving the rest of the band insane at rehearsals this week," she explained. "Chazza says he's changing the whole set around, *and* he did an interview with the college paper on his own, without telling the others it was happening. When they had a go at him about that, he told them that they should remember whose band it was!"

"Mmm – nice guy!" I winced, notching up another mental black mark against Linn's boyfriend in my head.

"Oh, yeah – and he's also been talking about changing the name of the band," Rowan began to tell me, just as we were interrupted by a scrabbling at her bedroom door.

"*Hola!*" Tor announced loudly, padding into the room clutching a white piece of paper. He plonked himself down on the duvet beside us.

"*Hola*, to you too, Tor!" smiled Rowan. "What can we do for you? Do you want your toenails painted, same as us?"

Tor leant over and studied both our sets of bare feet, then shook his head.

"So ... anything you want to tell us, Tor?" I asked him.

"*Si!*" Tor grinned, holding up the white A4 sheet for us to study.

It was dramatically edged in black and red, with swirly, fancy copperplate writing on it.

"'This is to certify'" I read aloud – "'that Tor Love raised the staggering sum of £4.28 for the Hamster Rescue Association.' Oh, well done Tor! Did Michael give you this?"

"*Si!*" beamed Tor.

Aww ... how lovely is our neighbour? Michael must have run this "certificate" off on the computer in his surgery, after Tor and Freddie had solemnly handed over their "staggering" takings from the charity junk-sale at the weekend.

"Did Freddie get one too?" asked Rowan.

"*Si!*"

There was silence for a moment, as all three of

us gazed some more at this home-made symbol of Tor's success.

"So, apart from showing us this ... *magnificent* certificate, is there anything else you'd like to tell us, Tor?" Rowan turned and quizzed our kid brother. "Like maybe why you're speaking in Spanish?"

"Wait a minute – Grandma must have been teaching him," I pointed out. "She and Stanley are doing that class, aren't they? Is that it, Tor?"

"*Si!*"

"And are '*si*' and '*hola*' all you know how to say in Spanish, Tor?" asked Rowan.

"*Si!*" Tor nodded emphatically.

"Cool. But listen – what did you come to tell us?" I tried to coax out of him. "And in English, please."

"Tea's ready in ten minutes – but can one of you come down and give Grandma a hand," he blurted out.

"I'll go," I told Rowan, as I swung my legs off the bed. "You've got *that* lot to tidy up."

Rowan glanced down at the splattered old tray on her bed that was piled high with tools of her (nail art) trade: assorted varnishes and paints and stained cotton-buds.

In a flash, she picked up the tray, leant over to the far side of her bed and clattered it down on the floor, out of sight.

"Ta-na! Tidy!" she beamed. "I'll come down-stairs with you..."

Now see: what Rowan had just done was a perfect example of why our house is the burglar-repulsing junk-heap it is ... i.e. it's what makes it *home*.

"So, what's Grandma making for tea tonight?" Rowan asked Tor, as we followed him down to the kitchen.

"Pie!" Tor called out, as he caught sight of Winslet trotting past with one of his wellies in her mouth and gave chase.

"It's paella, actually," said Grandma, as we joined her in the kitchen.

"The Spanish theme continues!" Rowan grinned, as she cast her eyes over the fancy-looking rustic bread in the middle of the table.

"Well, it just makes a change," said Grandma, stirring brusquely at something very garlicky in the frying pan. "Now, can one of you girls set the table for me, please? And set an extra place – Linn phoned to say she's bringing that Q boy back for tea."

Rowan and I froze.

Sensing the importance of our silence with her highly developed grandchild radar, Grandma spun round from the cooker and stared at us both.

"What?" she asked, darting her eyes at each of us in turn. "Don't you like Linn's friend?"

Grandma had an edge to her voice. Usually she plays it cool, calm and collected (while the rest of us are whirling around with severe cases of the emotional collywobbles), but now she was definitely taking notice. (Put it this way: if she was a dog, her ears would have pricked up.)

After all, this would be the first time she and Dad had met Q the Quite Horrible. *And* it was the first time any one of us Love children had brought a boyfriend home...

"No, we don't like him, do we, Al?" said Rowan, not bothering to mince her words.

"Um, no. Not really," I shrugged.

"Why not?" asked Grandma, interrogating us over the top of her glasses in her best *Weakest Link* impersonation.

"He's a big-headed git!" Rowan proclaimed succinctly.

But our rant to Grandma came to an abrupt halt as we heard the front door squeak open and a babble of voices bundle in. Sounded like Linn and her big-headed git had run into Dad coming home from work.

"OK, girls," Grandma whispered tersely to us both. "I want to see some polite behaviour tonight.

Maybe this boy didn't leave you girls with a very good first impression, but if Linn likes him, then he must have his good points."

You wanna bet, Grandma?

There was a strange little noise – only *just* in hearing range – going on in the kitchen. It was like a weird, low *hum* sort of a noise, but I didn't have the brain capacity to try and work out what it was exactly; too much else was going on around the kitchen table tonight...

"Oops!" murmured Tor, as he shook the ketchup bottle too hard and accidentally ended up with a great puddle of red *ooze* on his plate.

Speaking of food, Tor had only been *slightly* disappointed that he'd got tonight's menu wrong – although he wasn't too convinced by the olive bread (he spent quite a while picking all the bits of olive out and piling them up by the side of his plate), he was pretty taken with the paella when he realized that it was much easier to mould into a variety of interesting shapes than pie.

While our bruv was happily throwing himself into the finer points of food sculpting, Rowan and I decided to take a leaf out of Tor's book and be polite ... in a very silent way. Not that Q seemed to notice; he had eyes for only one person around the table – and it *wasn't* Linn.

"More paella, um … Q?" asked Grandma, holding a big blue ceramic bowl out towards him.

But instead of smiling, saying "Yes, please" and taking the bowl from her (like a normal person), Q just helped himself, while Grandma's arms began to shake under the weight of it. And while he was busy treating her like a Victorian serving wench (i.e. blanking her), he carried on his one-to-one conversation with Dad.

"Our music's like … like Limp Bizkit crossed with the Chili Peppers crossed with Stone Temple Pilots crossed with Ash. Know what I mean?"

"Um, kind of!" Dad shrugged across the table at Q, not having expected his simple question about Annihilator's musical style to have such a complicated answer. "Um, are you all right there, Irene?"

"Don't mind *me*, Martin," Grandma replied, tight-lipped, clattering the bowl on to the middle of the table when Q was done. It looked like she might be finding it a *teeny* bit difficult to take her own advice and be polite – since Q certainly wasn't bothering to be polite to her or anyone else, apart from Dad, it seemed.

What was all that about?

"So what was *your* band called, Mr Love?" Q slurped, through a mouthful of food.

(Mmm – Q was one of those people who eat with their gobs wide open; you could see the rice whirling around his mouth like laundry through the glass door of our washing machine.)

"Oh, call me Martin, please!" Dad smiled slightly nervously, while shooting a puzzled look around the table at his strangely silent family. "Anyway, we didn't get round to giving ourselves a name. In fact it was so long ago now that I can hardly remember the names of the other lads in the band!"

Dad's laugh spluttered to a halt when he realized that no one but Q and Linn were smiling at his joke-ette.

"Yeah?" grinned Q. "But I bet you were a *great* guitar player!"

Hark, is that the sound of someone sucking up? Someone sucking up *big* time?

"Me? *Nooo!*" beamed Dad, slightly bemused by all the attention and compliments coming his way. "I think I wasted my time buying such a good guitar in the first place – I never learnt to play much more than a couple of chords on it!"

Honestly, the band talk between Q and Dad had been going on *for ever*. It was so dull, it almost made me *pine* for that truly tedious documentary about the stags in Scotland. I was almost *thrilled* when I dropped my fork and had to bend down to get it – it gave me a chance to get away from the monotony of music banter for a bit. What it also did was give me the chance to find out what was behind the weird humming noise. There – under the table – was Winslet, staring directly at Q's jean-clad legs and keeping up a quiet, steady growl under her breath.

"Linn says it's a great guitar!" I heard Q gush, and I sat bolt upright again.

"Well, it is a vintage Fender Jaguar. I got it second-hand, but it still cost me a fortune at the time," Dad ruminated, with a far-off, nostalgic look in his eyes.

"Wow – a Fender Jaguar!" Q nodded. "And Linn was telling me it's still in mint condition, up in the attic!"

Linn – who'd been alternating between nibbling at her food and gazing adoringly at Q – managed to join in at this point.

"Q's up for learning to play guitar, Dad!" she piped up. "He wants to broaden his scope in the band, don't you?"

Across the table, I spotted Rowan rolling her kohl-lined eyes.

"Um, Q, dear," interrupted Grandma, "wouldn't you be more comfortable if you took your sun-glasses off?"

"Y'see, Martin," Q blustered on regardless, "*I* think it's important to be seen as a musician, and not just a singer. Y'know what I mean?"

(That look on Grandma's face? It was *identical* to the tight-lipped scowl Alfie was wearing on Sunday, in the café forecourt at the zoo.)

"Um, I suppose so," replied Dad, with a little frown flashing on to his forehead.

Poor Dad; he's totally gullible (same as my mum). He always believes people are innocent until proven guilty, or – more accurately, in this case – that people are nice and kind and good unless they do something radical to prove him wrong. Right at this minute, I think he was trying to work out whether Q was just being boyishly tactless (like boys generally are), or if he was being downright rude to Grandma.

"And so Q really needs a guitar to practise on!" Linn suddenly twittered, dropping a hint as heavy a ten-tonne truck.

Aha! So this was why she'd invited Q to tea! And this was why Q was buddying up to Dad! They both wanted him to hand over his guitar with love and best wishes – and, knowing what a softie he is, Dad was pretty likely to be suckered into doing just that, worse luck…

"Really?" Dad nodded, as he began refilling

everyone's glasses from a pitcher of orange juice, starting very pointedly with Grandma's glass. "Well, Q, from my own experience, I think you're best off with a simple acoustic guitar when you're starting out, not an electric one, like mine. But you probably know that already, you being in a band and everything."

Nice one, Dad! He'd managed to slither away from Linn's not-too-subtle request *super*-smoothly. And speaking of slithering, the smile on Q's face seemed to be slithering southwards now that he'd sussed that the Fender wasn't forthcoming.

"Uh, yeah ... sure," mumbled Q, blinking rapidly behind the darkened lenses of his stupid sunglasses.

And ooh – speaking of *smiles* – was that a little hint of a smirk appearing at the corner of my gran's mouth? Oh, yes – it definitely looked like Grandma might be the newest recruit to the Q Non-Fan Club. Not to mention Dad. Or Winslet.

Wonder if Tor could get some badges made up?

Chapter 16

MORE GROWLING IN THE KITCHEN...

"'*Hola!*' Oh – so she's in Spain this time, is she?" Sandie asked me, glancing up from the scribbled message she'd begun reading out loud.

"Uh-huh," I nodded.

It was Friday, Sandie was staying for tea (and the night), and I was showing her the letter (well, snapshot in an envelope) that had arrived from Mum this morning. Tor had been ecstatic when he'd seen that '*hola*' – he couldn't get over the coincidence of Mum being in Spain, just when he'd become practically bilingual. (Ha!)

"'Here's a photo of me,'" Sandie continued to read aloud, "'on the beach in Almeria – that's right down in the south of Spain, so close to Africa that you can see across the sea to Morocco on a clear day. Anyway, I'm working flat out at the moment, so I'll write more next time. Promise! Love to all my lovely Love children... Mum xxxxx (and save one of those kisses for Dad!)'"

Once she'd finished, Sandie flipped the photo

around and stared at the vision of my mother, grinning away with her long, wavy hair blowing in the wind, a sarong tied around her tanned legs and one of her own hand-printed T-shirts pulled over her chest. (It had a bluey-greeny design on the front that looked like it *might* be a jellyfish, or a fat starfish, or maybe just an amoeba or something.)

"Your mum – she's always so trendy..." Sandie sighed.

I always like the way my mother looks – all hippy round the edges – but I don't think she's really what you'd call *trendy*. For a start, she's always dressed like she's just stepped out of a seventies timewarp, and I don't think you'll see one of her amoeba T-shirts featured on the fashion pages of *Elle* any time soon. But then, I guess, compared to Sandie's mother (who puts the "mumsy" in mum), I know *my* mum comes across like Stella McCartney...

"Hmm ... tea should be ready soon," I pointed out, leaving fashion matters behind, since a rumble in my tummy was alerting me to the fact that it was nearly food o'clock. "Let's go downstairs..."

Sandie shrugged, and pushed herself up off my bed where she'd been sprawled, sticking the photo down on to my bedside table. (Later, I'd work out where Almeria was on the big map of the world that takes up practically a whole wall in my room. Would I stick a pin in to show where Mum was? *Si!*)

"You know something? I think my mum's fashion sense is getting worse – if that's possible," Sandie moaned, following me down the attic stairs. "Like, this week, I've been going on at her about how groovy Mel B and Posh Spice looked when *they* were pregnant –"

"*And* Madonna," I chipped in, turning on to the first-floor landing.

"– *and* Madonna. Exactly! But oh *no*; *my* mum goes and buys all these naff maternity tents."

Yeah – so these days Mrs Walker *did* tend to look like she'd stepped out of the shower and slipped on a *marquee*. But somehow I didn't really fancy seeing her parading her big bump around our local Budgens supermarket in a crop-top and crotch-hugging cargo pants. It would be a bit like Prince Charles turning up to state functions in a pair of flip-flops and a Union Jack thong.

I was still smiling to myself about marquees and thongs when I stopped at the top of the last set of stairs, that led down to the hall.

Two things had stopped me in my tracks (and made Sandie step on my heels and squeak "What's wrong?"). And those two things were...

1) The fact that Rowan, Tor and Rolf were all crouched on the very bottom step, huddling in a very suspicious manner, and...

2) There was the distinct sound of yelling drifting from the kitchen.

"What's going on?" I whispered, after tippety-toeing down smartish to join Ro & Co.

"Grandma and Linn – they're having a big ruck!" Rowan turned and whispered to me and Sandie, as the two of us huddled on the next step up from her and the boys.

"What about?" I asked in hushed tones.

"Q," Tor murmured darkly.

Y'know, I could have *sworn* Rolf gave a little growl at the sound of that name. Had he and Winslet been talking?

"What about Q?" I hissed at Tor.

"Linn asked Grandma what she thought of him," Rowan answered instead.

Oh...

"Grandma said he was *rude*!" Tor blurted out, obviously glad that his granny had seen the light.

"Yeah, Tor, but she did *try* to say nice things at first," Rowan whispered in explanation.

"*Are* there nice things to say about Q?" I muttered.

"Well ... she said he had nice teeth," Rowan shrugged.

Poor Grandma – she was really scraping the bottom of the barrel for compliments there. And poor Linn – you don't really want to hear that the best thing someone can say about your boyfriend is that he has nice *teeth*.

No wonder it had descended into a full-on barney…

"Listen!" whispered Sandie, her eyes as saucer-shaped as they get.

The voices were louder; the fighting – as they say on *News at Ten* – had escalated.

"You didn't even *try* to get on with him last night!" we all heard Linn shriek, in a desperate, wobbly voice.

"Linn, dear – *he* didn't try to get on with any of *us*, as far as *I* could see. Except for your father," Grandma retaliated.

"Huh!" hiccuped Linn. "Well, maybe that's because *Dad*'s the only one willing to give him a chance!"

"Yeah, but he wasn't exactly willing to give him his guitar!" Rowan whispered to the rest of us with a fleeting grin.

"That's as may be," we heard Grandma continue. "But I just think—"

"It doesn't *matter* what you think! It's what I *feel*! And I *love* him – OK?"

"Linn! Don't be silly!" we heard Grandma call out, as Linn stomped out of the kitchen. "You can't say you love someone after only two weeks!"

Linn didn't reply – at least, I didn't hear if she did.

After zooming upstairs at the speed of light, I couldn't hear anything for the sound of five thudding heartbeats (mine, Ro's, Sandie's, Tor's and Rolf's) as we hid together behind Rowan's bedroom door...

Chapter 17

ALL DRESSED UP AND NOWHERE (MUCH) TO GO

Sandie's grandparents had arrived for a visit today, which meant she was missing out on all the fun me and Kyra were having.

Ha.

"Omigod!" gasped Kyra. "The band are coming on stage! This is *so* exciting!"

Kyra didn't *look* too excited, and her voice was positively *dripping* with sarcasm.

"Hey, you wanted to hear them, didn't you?" I pointed out to her, as the roar of the crowd was replaced by an out-of-tune guitar twang.

"Yeah," scowled Kyra. "It's just that I kind of assumed we'd be *seeing* them too!"

Seemed like Kyra didn't think too much of my compromise.

I remember Dad once telling us kids that if all the politicians and stuff around the world learnt to compromise, then the world would be a much happier, calmer place. (I think the reason he was telling us this was because he'd overheard Linn and

Rowan arguing about whose turn it was to empty the bin or clean the loo or de-flea the cats or something.)

So, here's the way I figured it: Kyra was desperate to go to Annihilator's gig, while there was no way I wanted to go through the whole getting-smuggled-in-and-getting-chucked-out thing. (Can you imagine Grandma's face if she found out I'd spent the night in jail and been charged with Being Very Under Age in a Public Place?)

Anyway, after a week of worrying about falling out with Kyra over the gig business, I'd woken up in the middle of last night with a cat on my chest and a compromise in my head. Kyra and I *were* going to go to the gig – we just weren't going to go into the *building*.

"This was such a lousy idea," muttered Kyra, gazing around the alley we were standing in. "I mean, look – I bought new stuff to wear and everything, and we're spending our Saturday night in the college rubbish dump!"

I wouldn't exactly call it a *rubbish* dump. OK, the alley round the back of the college wasn't exactly Dettol-fresh, but at least it didn't have any age restrictions.

"Yeah – but we can still listen to the songs from here!" I said, pointing about three metres above our heads to the opened windows of the Student Union.

Kyra crossed her arms across her spangly pink bandeau top and narrowed her eyes at me.

"I thought we were going to be hanging out with the band!" she moaned. "Not hanging out with a bunch of smelly bins!"

She sulkily kicked an empty can with the toe of her cork wedge sandals, and then groaned as a trickle of sticky Pepsi splashed on her foot.

So much for my compromise. Kyra was *not* a happy bunny.

"Hey – I just thought of something!" I announced, as my brain clunked into gear.

"What?" snarled Kyra. "You want to go and check out all the skips in the neighbourhood after this?"

"Nah – I've just thought of a way we could watch the band," I replied, eyeing up what Kyra was wearing and wondering if my plan could work. Her black knee-length satiny skirt was so tight that she'd had to take diddy baby steps along the pavement tonight. How she could scramble up on top of a normal bin, then on to a big industrial dump bin, *then* on to a wall, I didn't know.

But I was forgetting what a determined (i.e. stubborn) person Kyra Davies is. Once I'd suggested that we could maybe see into the Student Union from the wall, Kyra had hitched up her skirt almost high enough to see her knickers, kicked her sandals off and held them between her teeth by the straps, and scrabbled up the bins like a mountain goat in a boob tube.

"They're pretty rotten," she announced half an hour later, as we sat perched on top of the wall, our legs dangling.

"Told you," I shrugged, peering in at the band thundering away under the spotlights in the crowded, darkened hall.

To be honest, I hadn't really been listening to the last couple of tracks (there wasn't any point – they all sounded the same: noisy, shouty and tune-free). Instead I'd been getting my insides all of a flutter at the idea that maybe Alfie was somewhere in that dark hall. If he and Linn were still speaking, of course. I'd no idea what was going on with the two of them since Linn had let Q snub him last Sunday…

"When are they going to play *your* song?" asked Kyra, swinging her sandals back and forth in her hand.

"Don't know," I replied, wondering how Rowan was feeling about it right now. She'd probably be standing somewhere down by the stage with Von, biting her sunflower nails to the quick with nerves. (Not her toenails, I mean – she'd done her finger-nails to match.)

"Thangyouverymuch," Q's voice mumbled murkily through the speakers, as the band lurched to the end of a track. "Some of you might know us as Annihilator, but just to let you know – as from tonight, the band's name is Q…"

"*What?!*" I squeaked, marvelling at the guy's cheek. We were too far away to check out the expressions on the faces of the other lads, but I'd have put a very large bet on the fact that they were scowling…

"…and anyway, this is our last song, and it's a slow one. Hope you like it!"

"Here it is! Here it is!" burbled Kyra, practically dropping her sandals on to the bins below in her excitement. And while Kyra burbled, I felt my breath go in and out in shallow hiccups as I waited to hear "Not Enough…".

To be honest, I didn't recognize the opening chords – but then, that was probably down to the fact that Q was playing them on his guitar, and the only time I'd heard it played before was when Chazza had strummed along to my warbling in the living room a couple of weeks back.

"*Ooh, babe,*" I heard Q begin to croon in a fake

American accent. "*You might be in ma bed, but you won't never get inside ma head.*"

Er … wait a minute.

"'*Won't never*'?" frowned Kyra. "That's not very good English, is it?"

"*An' though I got love for you, there's nothin' you can do, 'cause I'm a –*"

Q paused and did a quick, squealy guitar noodle before carrying on and yelping –

"*– FREEEEEE spirit! Ooh, yeah, babe, I'm a FREEEE spirit! Gonna say it again, 'cause I'm a FREEEEEE spirit!*"

My jaw had dropped so much that it was practically scuffing the floor of the alley.

"*I love you, baby, but I'm a FREEEE spirit – oooh, YEAH!*"

I suddenly became aware of Kyra's eyes *boring* into the side of my head.

"Did you write this poo?" she asked accusingly.

"Kyra, if I wrote this poo, do you *seriously* think I'd have dragged you down here to listen to it?" I raised my eyebrows at her.

"Well, what's happened to *your* song, then?"

How should I know? Q had gone and named the band after himself, so I guessed he was perfectly capable of replacing the slow, moody thing that me and Rowan had written with this icky, dodgy, slushy, gushy love song instead.

I sat stunned as he warbled through the rest of the track, and only shook myself back to life when Q plinked and plonked a last *twang!* or two on the guitar as his finale.

Um, speaking of guitars...

"Is that my *dad*'s guitar?" I gasped, recognizing the rounded black shape of the Fender from the fuzzy old photo that was now Blu-Tacked to my bedroom wall.

"He'd have been better with your brother's kazoo," Kyra grumbled. "He might have been able to play *that* in tune."

I wouldn't have minded getting my hands on Tor's kazoo now, so I could go and ram it right up the nose of Q the Quite Conniving...

Chapter 18

Q 4 LINN 4EVER (I DON'T *THINK* SO)

"Quick! Let's get out of here!" I heard Kyra whisper frantically.

Course, by the time I actually heard her words, the mountain goat in the boob tube had already bounded off the wall and was dropping herself down from the dumper and on to the bin.

"Wait for me!" I panicked, jumping on to the dumper's giant lid before spinning myself around and hoping my shaky arms would be strong enough to support me as I scrambled down on to the bin after her.

And the reason for this speedy descent? Well, there we were – Kyra and I – still perched on the wall, discussing just *how* Q had managed to get his slimy paws (no offence to our four-legged friends) on my dad's guitar, when all of a sudden an exit door in the building started making *thunking* noises, as if someone was trying to open it from the inside. I think it's safe to say that neither of us wanted to hang about and find ourselves chased out of the alley by irate security guards.

Clank!

Too late – the door had been thrown open.

"Uh ... need a hand there, girls?" I heard a male someone say.

"No, it's OK!" I heard Kyra giggle.

Giggling? At a security guard? Was that a good idea? Still, five out of five for Kyra's efforts at trying to *flirt* us out of trouble...

I stepped down from the bin on to the grotty alley floor, and – trying to suppress the jitters that were turning my legs to jelly – I turned round to see just how much trouble we were in.

And the answer was ... none.

The only trouble *I* was going to have was breathing, since the voice belonged to (oh, why hadn't I recognized it?) Alfie.

Uhhnunnnnggggahhhh...

"So ... what were you two, uh, doing up there?" he asked, blinking his long, feathery, fair eyelashes at us both in turn.

"Trying to watch the band. For free," Kyra grinned at him, trying to make the reason behind our gawping-from-a-distance sound a whole lot cooler than it actually was. "And what are you doing out here?"

Thank God for Kyra. Panic (at being handcuffed

by burly security guards) and shock (at seeing Alfie so unexpectedly) had sent a tidal wave of adrenaline shooting round my body. And until my currently soggy brain had drip-dried, the power of rational speech was beyond my control.

"Linn wanted to go backstage and see ... Q," he mumbled, with a couldn't-care-less shrug. Or maybe it was a can't-understand-why shrug. "There're loads of people just through there, hanging out with the band."

He nodded his lovely, spiky blond head towards the opened metal exit doors.

Sure enough, there seemed to be a hubbub of talking coming from a bundle of bodies just inside there somewhere. A few people (including a couple of band members) had stumbled out into the alley itself, armed with cans of beer and in search of fresh air.

"Is ... um, Rowan there?" I managed to choke out, just for something to say to Alfie.

"Yeah ... with that scary-looking mate of hers," Alfie nodded slowly.

That'd be Von, then.

"Is there a loo inside?" Kyra asked Alfie, as she bent down and fastened the sandals she'd slipped back on now that we were safely on terra firma (even if it was terra grotty firma).

"Yeah ... just go left, and they're at the end of the corridor," Alfie told her.

"Cool!" trilled Kyra, straightening up.

"Kyra!" I hissed, flashing her an alarmed glance.

"Back in a minute!" she grinned at me, flashing a heavy-duty wink in my direction.

Oh, yes – while Kyra was off noseying around at the band inside (the loo thing was just an excuse, I was positive), Kyra was sure she was doing me a humongous favour, leaving me all alone with Alfie. OK, so she knew how much I fancied him, but what she *didn't* know was quite how tongue-tied I got in his presence. Ah, for an unexpected eclipse to happen, so that this alley had the feel of the Twilight World – so dark that my nerves lost themselves somewhere in the shadows...

"So? What did you think of the ... um ... gig?" Alfie asked, as I resentfully watched Kyra scoot off inside the building.

(*Remember what you've learnt, Ally – five words or less; five words or less; five words...*)

"Hurumph," I murmured, screwing up my nose.

(I know, I know – technically "hurumph" isn't a word, but at least it wasn't a jumble of stammered twaddle either. And Alfie *seemed* to understand what I was trying to get across.)

"Yeah ... know what you're saying," he nodded slowly.

He did? Hurrah! Claim a miracle!

"I mean, that guitar-solo stuff Q was trying to do," Alfie leant forward and whispered conspiratorially. "How bad was that?"

"That," I quipped, finding my voice (and the English language) again "was my dad's guitar."

(A fine example of the Five Word Rule, I think you'll agree...)

"Yeah ... Linn told me it was your dad's," Alfie nodded, in that oh-so-sexy, hangdog way he has. "She said she'd borrowed it for him, 'cause Q really needed one."

"'Borrowed'?" I snorted. "That's not the word I'd use."

(Eek! More than five words! But look – still no stammering!)

"How come?" frowned Alfie.

(Ooh, that expressive frown – it was almost as gorgeous as any grin...)

"Linn must have sneaked the guitar out of the house without Dad knowing," I burbled, speaking way too fast but still not stumbling. "There's no *way* Dad would willingly let her take the Fender – not after turning her and Q down, the night he came round to ours for tea."

"Q came around to yours for tea?" Alfie blinked, as if this revelation showed just how horribly intimate Q had become in the life of Linn.

"Uh-huh," I nodded.

I watched as Alfie agitatedly ruffled his hands through his short spiky hair, keeping a close eye on his left hand in particular. After all, *that* was the hand that had held mine – even if it *was* for only a nanosecond, and even if it *was* by accident.

"God, she'd *never* do something like that on her own. That git's *made* Linn do it," Alfie growled. "And this all started that first night we met him."

Now it was my turn to frown – which Alfie (bless) noticed straight away.

"Remember that gig the band played in the pub on Holloway Road, Ally?" he asked me.

I nodded, *melting* to hear him use my name. But sure, of course I remembered that night – apart from it being the very first time I'd ever been (smuggled) into a pub, that was also the night Q somehow charmed my sister Linn into fancying him.

"Well, after you and Rowan left," Alfie began to explain, "he started flirting with Linn, chatting her up and stuff. Like I wasn't there. I mean, I could have been her boyfriend, for all he knew – or cared!"

I nodded again; that much I'd sussed.

"Anyhow ... he was just doing this stupid flirting thing, asking Linn if she liked the band and stuff," Alfie continued, checking over his shoulder for spies. "Then Linn mentions something about your dad having been in a band, and having a Fender ... thingy—"

"Jaguar," I butted in, helpfully, digging into my memory banks and remembering what Dad had called it.

"Yeah ... one of them," Alfie nodded, "and it all changed. Suddenly he got *really* interested in Linn."

As I watched those words leave Alfie's mouth, I was struck by three monumentous thoughts.

1) So, was *that* what Linn's appeal was for Q? Not that she was pretty, or smart, or sussed or anything – it was 'cause she had access to something he wanted. How shallow and sneaky was that?

2) How on earth (never mind the entire universe) could I get Linn to see what was going on?

3) How could I stop myself from supergluing my lips to Alfie's since his gorgeous face was so, so, *so* very close to mine right that second?

"Ally!"

"Ro!" I exclaimed, setting eyes on my twinkling sister.

Rowan had glitter sprinkled on her crimped hair, smeared on her eyelids, her cheekbones and her shoulders. Apart from that, she was wearing a black spaghetti-strap vest and a short denim skirt – pretty plain until you looked at the denim jacket she was holding. She'd unpicked the pink-sequin heart that had been on it last time I'd seen it, and sewn on a corsage of fabric sunflowers (to match her nail art) instead.

"I just saw Kyra inside in the queue for the loos," she said, hauling her customized jacket on now that she'd realized she was in the breezy outdoors. "She said you two had come down to try and hear our song."

At that, she rolled her eyes so much that a few flecks of glitter fluttered from her eyelids and down on to her cheeks. Which was a nice effect, actually.

"So, why did they do that other cruddy song instead?" I asked her.

Alfie snickered when I said that; honest he did. *How* cool...

"Omigod, Ally, the rest of the band are just *furious* with Q," she gushed. "They'd rehearsed 'Not Enough...' all week, and then at rehearsal this afternoon Q turns up with that stupid 'Free Spirit' song he'd written and announces they're going to do *that* instead."

"What about the name change?" Alfie butted in, looking like he was loving this bitchy gossip about Q. (Wow, that guy must really have got under Alfie's skin – Alfie is just *so* not the bitchy-gossip type.)

"Total surprise!" said Rowan, throwing her hands palms-up in the air so that all her bracelets rattled. "When he announced it on stage, that was the first they'd heard of it! And when they came off stage, the other lads all had to hold Chazza back to stop him *thumping* Q!"

"Heh, heh, heh!"

(That was Alfie, by the way. I guess thoughts of thumping Q had entered *his* head too.)

"And did you know that was Dad's guitar, Ro?" I pointed out.

"Chazza told me – I couldn't believe it!" she replied, shaking her head in astonishment. "And I can't believe Linn could have lent that louse Dad's guitar. Sorry, Alfie – I know she's your mate and everything!"

Alfie just shrugged. Obviously, his and Linn's friendship was on rocky ground at the moment.

"And that's why I want to leave right now," Rowan announced, hugging her denim jacket close around her. "I can't handle being around Linn, to be honest. Von's going to hang about and get a lift home with Chazza, but I just don't want to be here for a second longer, not with Q and Linn swanning around like they're the rock-band version of Posh and Becks or something. Coming, Ally?"

"I can't – there's Kyra," I mumbled, pointing in the direction I'd last seen my friend going in.

"It's OK – I said as much to her a second ago," Rowan told me. "She said she'll be right out."

As if on cue, Kyra sashayed out of the exit, shooting a huge, wide-eyed "Well?" look in my direction, as if me and Alfie might have snogged and set the date for our *engagement* or something while she'd been away.

"Hey, I'll come with you guys," Alfie mumbled. "Can't say I fancy hanging around here either..."

"OK!" I said brightly, already plotting how I could wangle sitting next to him on the bus. Then I hesitated, noticing three sets of eyes staring at me.

Hmm. Remember this for the future, Ally: yelping "OK!" at a trillion decibels is NOT cool... I muttered silently inside my head.

Chapter 19

MISSING! THE LOVE FAMILY'S BRAINS...

Well, from the debris scattered around, it looked like Tor and Dad had had a *rockin'* Saturday night.

The entire living-room floor was covered in click-together plastic racetrack, so a mini-Grand Prix had obviously taken place. Interestingly enough, part of the race circuit went through a set-up game of Mousetrap. I'd spotted all that (tripped *over* all that) last night when Rowan and I arrived home, but when I tramped down to the kitchen this morning, I saw that the festivities had spilt through to the back of the house, too.

There were two empty pizza boxes beside the sink (empty of *pizza*; a purring cat that wasn't Colin was curled up in one of them). The table was covered with crumbs, an empty two-litre bottle of Irn Bru, plus glasses, and a giant jigsaw puzzle of a rhinoceros, which wasn't quite finished – maybe 'cause Dad and Tor had been too distracted by the tent thing they seemed to have constructed out of all six dining chairs and a Bob the Builder bedsheet.

It was just gone 9 a.m., and the tent – as well as every room downstairs – was uninhabited, apart from random mutts, moggies and me. (Actually, the tent *was* inhabited – by Winslet, who was quietly chewing on a light snack of stray rhino-puzzle pieces.)

"Everybody still sleeping, are they, puss?" I muttered to the cat that wasn't Colin.

Lucky everybody else … I'd had a rubbish night's sleep, worrying about Linn's dubious taste in blokes (or at least, *bloke*); worrying about Linn biting my head off if I dared to tell her he was a creep; and wondering why Rowan had ended up sharing a seat next to Alfie on the bus home yesterday evening while I'd somehow ended up sitting behind them like Cinderella. With Kyra the human mountain goat, of course.

Ho hum.

As I yawned my way over to the kettle, I suddenly spotted a note taped to the jar where the teabags live. Focusing my sleep-bleary eyes on Dad's scrawl, I mumbled his message out loud.

Dear Whoever Gets Up First –
I'm off down to the police station. Don't panic! I

haven't committed any heinous crimes during the night. It's just that I got a call this morning to say that a whole bunch of stolen stuff has turned up in a burglary suspect's flat, and they need me to come down to the station and see if any of it's ours. I tried to tell them that nothing was taken when we got broken into, but they just want to make sure.

Back soon – and leave some Crunchy Nut Cornflakes for me!

Love Dad x

I stuck the note back on the jar and went to fill the kettle, then stopped. The police station wasn't far from ours – maybe I'd go round and meet Dad. It sure beat hanging around here with only my stupid thoughts, a jigsaw-chewing dog and a pizza-scented cat for company...

I'd thought that when I bumped into Dad, the most I'd see him carrying was a couple of Sunday papers. And maybe a new box of Crunchy Nut Cornflakes.

But as I stomped along the empty Sunday-morning streets towards the police station, I have to say I didn't expect to spot him padding towards me – in his Doc Martens, worn jeans and old grey T-shirt – balancing a heavy-looking cardboard box in one hand and pushing a half-built bike in the other.

"Hey, Ally Pally!" he called out to me. "Come to give me a hand?"

"What is all this stuff, Dad?" I asked, peering into the box as I drew level.

"Um, let's see..." he said, resting the box down on the pavement. "There's my radio; Rowan's watch; the clock from the mantelpiece; that antique vase that sat on the hall window sill with the plastic flowers in it; two of Mum's smaller paintings from the living room; Tor's rollerblades; Tor's box-set of *Toy Story* videos; two candlesticks; an old chequebook of mine that didn't have any cheques in it, thankfully; and, oh – this is yours, isn't it, Ally Pally?"

He pulled out a matted-looking Furby Baby, which promptly flipped open its eyes and let out an indignant "Eeeeoooowww!"

"Yeah – Sandie gave me that last Christmas," I nodded.

I hadn't seen it for ages. I just occasionally heard a stifled "Kah-a-tay! Kah-a-tay! Wah!" but never could figure out where Winslet had stashed the stupid thing. But it seemed like the burglars had managed to find it. Or maybe Winslet had presented it to them as they scrambled in through the smashed kitchen window – like the Native American Indians trustingly offering food and hospitality to Christopher Columbus & Co until their visitors gave them smallpox and nicked all their land off them.

"They took all this stuff?" I blinked at Dad. "And we never noticed?"

Dad scratched at the dark stubble on his chin, and nodded.

"Seems so…" he shrugged. "Maybe Linn's got a point – maybe the house *is* a bit messy, if we didn't even spot that anything was gone."

"And that?" I said, pointing to the saddleless, handlebarless bike.

"Oh, that was the one I was halfway through fixing up," Dad blinked, a bit of a blush of embarrassment on his cheeks. "I totally forgot about it, what with the upset of the house getting broken into and everything…"

God, what a useless family we were. No wonder Linn sometimes wanted to trade us in. Mind you, she had a useless boyfriend, so she couldn't be *too* smug.

"Dad…" I began, launching into what was on my mind as I grabbed the broken bike from him so that he only had to carry the box home.

"Oooh, that sounded like an ominous 'Dad'.

What's up?" he smiled, as we strolled along the street.

"What do you think of Q?" I asked, shielding my eyes with one hand against the morning sun.

"He's ... well, I'm sure he's all right, in his own way," Dad answered, in a typically well-meaning, non-committal Dad way. "Why are you asking, Ally Pally?"

"It's just ... it's just that *we* don't like him," I told him, biting my lip.

"Really?" he frowned a concerned frown. "Who's 'we'?"

"Well, me, Rowan, Tor, Grandma and Alfie," I reeled off, holding up my free hand and counting everyone off on my fingers. Course, there were a lot of people who didn't like Q, so I had to put my fingers back down one by one as more names sprang to mind. "And then there's Chazza and Von, and the other four lads in the band..."

"Hmm. That's quite a lot of people," Dad nodded thoughtfully. "And why doesn't anyone like him?"

"Well, he's really self-centred and rude," I started to explain.

"Oh," Dad murmured, not – I noticed – rushing to contradict me. "Still, Linn seems very fond of him."

"Yeah, well, that's the other thing about him – he's a user," I blurted out, working up to the news I was about to break.

"What? A *drug* user?" said Dad in a startled voice.

"God, no!" I assured him quickly. Maybe I didn't like Q, but I didn't want to accuse him of such a horrible habit, especially when he had *enough* faults to be going on with. "He's a *people* user."

"A what?" Dad frowned at me.

"A people user!" I repeated. "Me and Rowan and Alfie, we think – well, we *know* – that Q only got really interested in Linn when she told him about you and your guitar. 'Cause he fancied getting his hands on it, I mean."

"That can't be true, can it?" Dad asked, furrowing his dark eyebrows even more.

"Yeah! That's why Q was being so nice to you the other night!" I burbled on, feeling my heart pounding. "He was after your guitar – you *know* he was; you heard him hinting – so he turned on the charm! Only you knocked him back…"

Dad shrugged thoughtfully, but said nothing.

OK, it was time to bite the bullet and tell him the whole story.

"The thing is," I winced, "Linn lent him your guitar anyway."

I think I held my breath after I said that. What-ever, I felt pretty light-headed for a second, until I could see how Dad'd take the traitorous news.

"Oh."

"Oh"? Was that *all* Dad was going to say? Wasn't he *furious*?

"Aren't you mad at her?" I asked him out loud, studying his craggy, troubled-looking face.

"Yes..." he nodded slowly, still studying the pavement as we walked along. "And I guess I *will* have to have a talk with her –"

Poor Dad; he really hates it if he ever has to do the Stern Parenting Talk thing with any of us. I swear he finds it more cringe-worthy and upsetting than any of *us* do.

"– but I guess she *is* seventeen."

"So?" I shrugged in confusion.

What was so special about being seventeen? Did you get a special dispensation card on your seventeenth birthday or something? Could you be as bad-tempered and troublesome as you wanted and people would let you off?

"*So*, Ally Pally, being seventeen can be really difficult," Dad tried to smile at me. "I remember what it was like – you feel like you're totally adult, but you've got parents and maybe kid brothers and sisters breathing down your neck, making you feel restless and like *everyone* and *everything*'s holding you back. And then, added to that, you've got the pressure of big, scary exams. And if you happen to fall in love for the first time around then, too... Well, the stress of everything together can be tough!"

OK, now he was scaring me. *Now* I was going to spend the next four years *dreading* being seventeen, since it sounded like sheer misery...

"Don't get me wrong!" Dad suddenly burbled, clocking my worried expression and ruffling my hair with one hand (which was kind of nice and kind of annoying at the same time). "It's not that I'm making excuses for her – but I think sometimes Linn finds it hard, being the eldest one out of you lot, being the most responsible; specially with your mum not being around."

"Is that why she gets so moody sometimes?"

There – I'd asked it. The question that always preyed on mine and Rowan's minds.

"I think so. But she handles it all pretty well most of the time, doesn't she?"

"S'pose so," I muttered, thinking about the time Linn took charge of the spying mission on Dad when we'd all convinced ourselves that he'd got himself a new girlfriend (which he hadn't, of course; just a terrible new hobby – the dreaded line-dancing). Not to mention how she calmly helped Rowan solve the shoplifting mess she'd got herself into not so long ago. Yeah, I suppose she wasn't a narky old nagbag *all* the time...

"Well, I just think we've got to give Linnhe a little leeway now and again," Dad mused.

"You mean, you're going to let her off about lending Q your guitar without asking?" I checked with him.

"No," Dad shook his head. "I mean, I'll give her the chance to explain *why* she did what she did, as long as she understands that I'm not pleased that it happened. It's what I'd do for all of you, Ally Pally – you know that, don't you?"

I nodded silently as we trundled along for a few steps, me and my dad both thinking our own swirly thoughts, when another question popped into my head, and right out of my mouth.

"You know something?"

"Nope," Dad smiled at me.

"I wish the burglars had stolen your Fender wotsit," I told him.

"Really? Why?"

"'Cause you'd have got it back today, like all the rest of this stuff," I replied, nodding at the cardboard box he was carrying. "Instead of waiting till Linn gets it back off Q."

"Yes, but then you might have asked to hear me play something this afternoon," grinned Dad. "And then you'd understand why the band I was in never got beyond three rehearsals!"

"How bad were you?" I grinned back.

"Ally, put it this way – I played guitar as well as Rowan cooks..."

Aha... Rowan can set fire to soup. Rowan thinks tuna and peanut butter go really well together in a sandwich. Rowan once put frozen peas in a jelly, 'cause it made it "look more interesting". And last night, on the way home, Rowan had muttered something about experimenting with a Supernoodle omelette for our tea tonight.

Wow – Dad must have been a truly *terrible* guitar player...

Chapter 20

HARK! IS THAT THE SOUND OF LINN'S HEART BREAKING?

While Rowan, Tor and Winslet were busy inspecting the box of burgled bits with Dad, I took a deep breath and started climbing the stairs to the attic. Ever since I'd got home, I'd felt awful for telling Dad everything without confronting Linn myself first. Maybe if I could just talk to her before Dad had his little chat with her...

It was just that I knew I'd think of myself as a pretty rotten sister if I didn't tell Linn what a two-faced, scheming super-creep her boyfriend was, even though I knew what a *dead* sister I might be once I'd blabbed all that to her... Still, I had to try (I just wished my hand would stop shaking as I knocked at her door).

"Come in," came an unexpectedly wobbly voice.

"Linn?" I said softly, tiptoeing inside the hallowed ground of my sister's white sanctuary.

And there she was, in her white pyjamas, huddled up under her white duvet – with a pile of soggy, white paper tissues spread out all around her.

"What's wrong?" I asked, tentatively perching myself on the end of the bed, half-expecting Linn to roar at me to get off and stop creasing the duvet cover.

But she didn't – she just dabbed at her red-rimmed eyes and blew her runny, red nose. She still looked kind of pretty, though. (Curses.)

"Rowan'll be pleased," she mumbled, sounding a mixture of bitter and sad.

"Huh?" I frowned.

"She never liked Q, did she?"

Oh...

"Has, uh, something happened?" I asked vaguely, in case I'd somehow picked this up all wrong. But it *had* to be over between Linn and Q, didn't it? Why else would she be blubby and bitter?

"Yeah, you *could* say something happened. You *could* say I've been an idiot for trusting that *pig*," Linn sniffled. "You *could* say I've chucked him."

Yes! Hallelujah! Let's get bunting and streamers hung all over the house!

"But what happened? Why did you finish with him?" I pushed her, hoping I sounded calm and collected and not deliriously thrilled.

"You know how he played that gig last night?"

she said, unaware that I'd seen it all from a great height (i.e. the alley wall).

I nodded.

"Well, afterwards, I was hanging about backstage," Linn began to explain, pulling another tissue out of the box. "And Q just kept ignoring me, talking to other people and acting like I wasn't even *there*. It was as if –"

She hesitated, her voice cracking slightly, and her eyes filled with spill-friendly tears again.

"– he didn't care about me at all! Not now that he was busy posing with that stupid guitar!"

Quelle surprise, as they say in France.

"Here," I mumbled, passing her another tissue or three.

"And then I overheard him talking to this lad," she sniffled. "And Q was – he was telling him that I was 'not bad' to have as a girlfriend, but that the best thing about going out with me was getting his hands on Dad's prize Fender!"

I was about to gasp "No!" and feign surprise, but I'm rubbish at lying; I really am.

"Er … I know," I mumbled.

"What?" Linn squeaked. "What do you mean, you know!"

"Me and Rowan and Alfie – we figured it out from stuff Q said and did."

Linn opened and closed her mouth a couple of times, looking totally (and reasonably) confused.

"It was stuff like him sucking up to Dad the other night when he came round for tea," I tried to explain. "And then when I got talking to Alfie last night, he said you told Q about the guitar at that first Annihilator gig, and so it all kind of slotted together. He said that—"

"You were at the gig last night?" Linn blinked at me.

"Not *exactly*," I shrugged.

Then we both gave up and fell silent for a second; suddenly it didn't seem important for Linn to know all about me and Kyra hovering among the trash cans in the alley, just as it didn't seem important for Linn to know how we all knew that Q was a creep before she did.

"Um, Linn…" I began hesitantly.

"What?" she sniffled, red-eyed, at me.

"Well," I shrugged, "I've got *good* news and *bad* news."

"Better give me the bad news first, I suppose," Linn mumbled fatalistically.

"The bad news is…" I took a deep breath, "…Dad knows you lent Q the guitar without asking."

"How did he find out?" she gasped.

"I … uh … *I* told him. I recognized it when I saw

Q playing it last night," I mumbled pinkly.

"And you went and told *Dad*?!" Linn said accusingly.

"And you went and lent Q the guitar without *asking*?!" I retaliated.

It was Linn's turn to go pink. There was no point arguing – Linn knew she was in the wrong; her silence said as much.

"Oh God," she muttered after a few seconds, her head dropping down on to her knees. "He's going to be *so* mad at me, isn't he?"

"Nah … just a bit hurt," I tried to reassure her. "I think if you get it back quickly he won't freak out too much."

"But how can I do that?" Linn whined, raising her head and looking pitifully at me. "I can't bear being anywhere *near* Q. I never, ever want to see him again!"

For a second, I thought about suggesting that Rowan and I went to Q's house to demand the return of the Fender, but then I realized that there was someone who'd get a *much* bigger kick out of doing that favour for Linn.

"Alfie!" I announced. "Alfie will go and get it if you ask him!"

"I don't know about that…" Linn replied dubiously. "Alfie's gone a bit funny on me lately."

"He was just allergic to Q," I grinned at her. "He'll be fine now he knows you've finished with him."

"Do you think so?"

I nodded enthusiastically, and stretched over to grab her mobile off her table.

"Call him and see!" I told her brightly.

"Hmm..." murmured Linn, her finger hovering over the buttons.

"Oh – don't you want to know the good news?" I suddenly asked her, before she got a chance to dial.

"Go on, then," Linn replied, smoothing her hair behind her ears now that she was feeling more composed.

"Dad says we're going to have a huge spring clean of the house!" I announced. "You know – chuck out loads of stuff!"

For a second, Linn's face brightened, then she wrinkled her nose and smiled wryly.

"Yeah, I'll believe *that* when I see it! Getting this house tidy is about as likely as the Queen turning Buckingham Palace into a B&B!" Linn scoffed, as she turned her attention to the phone again.

"Um, Linn..." I interrupted her, before she'd got a chance to key in Alfie's number.

I'd come up here to get things sorted with her,

and since Linn hadn't sent me packing or torn my head off, I decided I might as well get something else off my mind.

"What?"

"Well," I began, twisting a chunk of duvet cover around between my fingers (which I stopped doing when I noticed Linn watching me). "You've been really grumpy lately, and ... and Dad says it's because you're seventeen. Only, that can't be right because you're always a bit grumpy. And you were grumpy when you were sixteen too. *And* when you were fifteen. *And* when you were—"

"Ally," Linn interrupted me wearily. "I don't know what point you're trying to make, but the phone's ringing, OK?"

Linn held up her mobile so I could hear the distant trilling at Alfie's end.

"OK," I muttered, getting to my feet now that I realized I was dismissed. Seemed like talking about Linn's grumpiness was just getting her grumpy again. And it had been going *so* well...

"Oh, hi, Alfie! It's me," I heard my sister say, as I backed myself out of her room and pulled the door closed behind me. "I was calling 'cause ... actually, hold on a sec. *Ally!*"

"Yep?" I said hesitantly, peering back around the door to see what I'd done wrong now.

"Look," Linn said hurriedly, holding her hand over the phone. "Sometimes it's hard for me. Sometimes, I just feel like the odd one out in this family. OK?"

She clocked my questioning expression (my *dumb* expression) and sighed.

"You and Rowan and Tor and Dad – you're all so alike. Even Mum. Sometimes I don't feel like I belong. Specially when Dad and Tor are so close, and you and Ro are hanging out together all the time. Get it?"

Oh.

I'd never thought that Linn could be jealous of me and Ro being buddies (specially since the reason we got on was because we were united in our fear of Linn's grouch moments).

And I'd never thought for a nanosecond that I was anything *like* my airhead sister or my spooky brother or my dear old dopey dad (or even my lovely long-gone mum). But I guess if you were from the Planet Zarg, you'd probably assume that the four of us messy, dark-haired doughballs (excluding Mum) were related, and might presume that the immaculate, well-ironed, blonde-haired girl was just visiting.

Poor Linnhe Love – the rest of us (specially me and Ro) would have to try *really* hard not to make her feel left out. And that could start with keeping her happy, even if that meant the ultimate sacrifice – keeping the house tidy.

"Got it!" I nodded at Linn, closing the door softly and letting her get back to Alfie.

A passing cat that wasn't Colin frowned as I spat on my sleeve and wiped my greasy fingerprints off the doorknob.

"Got to start somewhere, puss!" I said cheerfully, just as the cat that wasn't Colin began retching, and barfed up a furball right outside Linn's room...

Chapter 21

PASS THE EARPLUGS, PLEASE

"What's the name of this lot?" came a voice from a table right behind us.

"Uh, I think it's on the poster right behind them," came another voice. "Let's see; they're called ... Nutter."

Maybe I should have turned around and set those people straight; told them that the poster said NNHLTR (aka Annihilator), but I kind of thought Nutter suited them better, somehow.

I don't think the other customers in the pub were really enjoying the thrash metal that the band were playing. Dad said that this pub usually has gentle, fiddlee-i-di-do Irish music, or pretty, pringly-prangly Spanish-guitar stuff during their regular Sunday lunchtime concerts (kids welcome).

Still, the Love family (& Co) were here to show support. Dad was slapping the table with his hands (keeping time a lot better than the actual drummer), Rowan was beaming with pride (ditto Von, sitting next to her), I was entertaining myself by watching

Billy wince beside me as we listened to Chazza howl out lyrics (oh, yes – he was the lead singer now!), while Tor sat happily making a log cabin out of the French fries that came with his burger.

Linn was here, too – mainly because Q wasn't – and was sitting at the table next to the rest of us, with (sigh!) Alfie.

So, I guess you'll have spotted it wasn't just *Linn* who had dumped Q. After last week's gig at the college, Chazza and the other lads decided they'd had enough, and politely suggested to Q that he might like to take his new band name, his rotten guitar playing, his even *more* rotten slow song, and get lost. Actually, the way Rowan tells it, I think it came out a *lot* ruder than that.

Yep, it was official – Q had managed to show himself to *everyone* as the slug he was (no offence to slugs, who'd probably make much better boy-friends than Q). What was *also* official was Q's real name… Now that she'd dumped him, Linn was happily spilling Q's biggest secret: that the name on his birth certificate was the very un-rock'n'roll Brian Clump. He'd given himself the nickname Q after the title of a music magazine. Pity there wasn't a magazine called *Prat*…

A crashingly loud guitar chord brought the current track to an end, and nearly shook the fillings out of my teeth. (The guitar, by the way, was Dad's Fender – rescued by Alfie from the odious Brian, and now on long-term loan, with Dad's blessing, to the far more deserving and appreciative Chazza.)

"Hi," Chazza mumbled into the microphone between numbers. "We're going to quieten things down a bit now –"

"Thank God for that!" I heard a disgruntled voice mumble at the table behind us.

"– with a new song. But we need a little help for this one. Girls?"

Tor stopped playing with his chips and joined me, Dad, Linn, Billy and Alfie as we gawped at Rowan and Von, who'd just giggled their way over to join the band.

"Is Rowan actually going to *sing*?" Billy murmured incredulously in my ear.

"Please, God, no…" I murmured back. It's not as if Rowan has the *worst* voice in the world, but let's put it this way – having her warbles amplified through a microphone wasn't exactly going to do her any favours. If there were any music producers in the audience today, I couldn't really see them rushing for their chequebooks to sign her up. Rushing for the door, maybe…

"Um … hello!" Rowan blushed into a microphone, going nearly as red as the fake roses she'd sewn into a bangle around her wrist. "This one's called 'Not Enough...', and I'd like to, well, I'd like to –"

Uh-oh. All of a sudden the hairs on my neck were standing to attention: not only was my sister about to sing in public (erk!), but it also looked like Rowan was going to tell the world (OK, the twenty people in this pub) that little old me had had a hand in writing this particular song...

Wow.

"– I'd just like to dedicate it to my sister Ally."

And with that, the band cranked into the tune, with Chazza crooning out the first line, while Rowan and Von harmonized (i.e. went "Ahhh, ahhh!" a bit) in the background.

"You smile, but it makes me shiver,
You look my way and it makes me shake,
Every time you talk to me
I'm sure it's just some mistake..."

Maybe the band line-up had changed, but it looked like Rowan still worried about the boys being phobic about thirteen-year-old songwriters in their midst. Ah, well, maybe it wasn't so bad that Rowan hadn't spilt the beans – not with Alfie sitting close enough to feel the heat of embarrassment radiating from my body when I listened to the words: words that had started out being about Billy and his lost love and turned out to be about me and Alfie really.

"...'Cause I know you like me,
Just not enough,
Not enough,
Not enough..."

I couldn't resist it – I had to peek at Alfie, to see if by some miracle the words were casting a love charm over him and making him fall flat on his face in love with me, or to see if that hand of his was creeping towards mine for another, illicit clasp.

Nope.

The grin and the thumbs-up he gave me? That was matey: that was one mate showing another mate how chuffed he was that we were sitting here with Linn, who'd come back to us – and back to her senses.

Still, at least Alfie seemed to see me as an almost-mate now – not just as Linn's semi-invisible kid sister. And that can't be bad...

Oh, and speaking of Linn returning to her senses, she'd also returned to her old, grouchy self...

"Is Ro *deliberately* trying to bring shame to this family?" she leant over and whispered to me.

"Just be glad the dogs aren't here," I grinned back.

Mind you, compared to the racket "Nutter" were making, maybe the other customers would have preferred the sweet, howling tones of Rolf and Winslet...

Till next time,
love + hugs + earplugs
Ally :c)

PS Chazza's band are doing pretty well now, but you won't find me sneaking under age into any venues to see them. Hanging around with Sandie and Billy and the rest of my mates is a lot more fun – and a lot less likely to give me an ulcer before I turn fourteen. Also – to be brutally honest – Annihilator suck.

PPS You know the business of the big house clear-out? Well, we did it – it took a whole weekend of hoovering and dusting and dragging crammed bin-bags of clutter to the charity shops, but we did it, much to Linn's amazement. The only thing is, I think she was *less* than chuffed when Dad, Rowan, Tor and I came back from a car-boot sale this Sunday with armloads of brand-*new* clutter to take its place. Ah – home, sweet (scruffy) home...

Coming soon:

Parties, Predicaments and Undercover Pets

It was Monday, it was about ten to lunch, and I'd just sat through a morning of talks from a variety of writers, in the company of a very weird mixture of people from my year (i.e. Feargal and Co, amongst others). I'm not sure why our normal classes were broken up and muddled together for these "Write On" sessions, but I'd found myself with only Kyra and Jen for close company. Who knows which writers Sandie, Chloe, Salma and Kellie were with, but I only hoped they were more interesting than the lot we'd been subjected to. I mean, a writer from the *Telegraph* newspaper, who was boasting about his prize-winning feature on the gross national product of Guatemala? *Please!* Had he mistaken us for a bunch of fifty-year-old businessmen? Had he mistaken us for people who cared?

And then there was the bloke who made up crosswords for national magazines. Fascinating. But not as fascinating as the woman who worked for

Concrete Today magazine. Or was it *Tarmac Monthly*? I can't remember, since I lost my will to live somewhere during her talk. No wonder Feargal O'Leary and his mates were acting up. Mind you, they *always* act up. They are, officially, the bad lads in our year – although no one seems very sure what bad things they get up to, other than cheeking the teachers and looking tough.

Feargal O'Leary looks the toughest of all the lads, even though they all wear identical hooded sweatshirts under their blazers (hoods worn up whenever possible), with matching slouches and scowls (when they're not snickering wickedly). But I've got a theory about Feargal and why he acts the way he does; I just reckon that it must be hard to be the leader of a tough boy gang when you're name is Feargal O'Leary – and you're black. Being lumbered with the name of an old, Guinness-drinking Irish bloke must be a pain in the neck when you're a cool young black guy. What were his parents thinking of? OK, so your parents can't help what your second name is (that's just a fact of long-lost family history), but "Feargal" for a first name? Even the Irish lads at our school think that's funny. It almost made me feel sorry for him...

"Anyway, after I left *Smash Hits*," Miss Gray continued, once Mr Samuels gave her a nod, "I found time to start writing this book, which I based on my teenage diaries. Does anyone here keep a diary?"

Oops – before I'd had time to think of the implications (i.e. looking like a total nerdy swot), my hand shot up in the air.

"*Pfffffttttt!*"

Of course, I couldn't be sure exactly where that jeering snicker came from, but I had a fairly good idea. So did Kyra, swinging round in her seat beside me and shooting daggers towards the rear of the class and Feargal's lot.

"Yes?" the woman smiled encouragingly at me.

"Go on, Al!" Jen whispered at me, nudging my ankle with her foot (ouch).

"I ... um ... don't keep a diary, exactly," I gulped, trying hard to sound confident, but sure I was failing miserably. "It's more of a ... a thing that I carry around with me to write stuff down in. Like a ... a..."

God, this was going to sound so pretentious.

"Like a what?" Miss Gray prompted me.

"A journal. Well, a journal thing. Kind of."

"*Pffffffttttt!*"

Urgh.

"Really?" Mr Samuels nodded at me. "And what do you keep in this journal, Ally?"

"Um ... I just scribble things in it, things people say, or what I'm thinking..."

"*Pfffffftttttt!*"

"...and I write down bits out of my favourite songs..."

"*Pfffffffffffffffftttttttt!*"

"...and bits of poems," I blushed, wishing I'd never stuck my stupid hand anywhere except across my mouth. I'd only started the stupid thing yesterday – it was hardly a life-long passion. What did I have to go and talk about it in front of everyone for?

"*Pfffffffftttttttttttttttttttttttttttttt!*"

"You lot! Enough!" Mr Samuels barked in Feargal's direction.

"Your own poems, er, Ally, isn't it?" Miss Gray carried on regardless (though I wish she hadn't bothered).

"Some..." I shrugged miserably. "Some by real poets too."

"Have you got it with you now?" Miss Gray smiled at me.

"Yes..." I replied dubiously, curling my fingers around the soft cover of the small notebook in my blazer pocket.

Oh, good grief – she wasn't going to ask me to read something from it, was she? *Please* let Martians beam me out of this classroom, *please* let

Martians beam me out of this classroom...

"Well," beamed Miss Gray, whom I was really beginning to dislike, "I'm sure we'd all love to hear—"

The bell! The glorious, ear-splitting *Braannggg!!!* was music to my ears! Me and my stupid journal were spared!

"I'm sure everyone would like to thank Miss Gray for a very interesting and informative talk!" yelled Mr Samuels over the screech of chairs as everyone bolted for the door and lunch.

"Thank you, Miss Gray," I mumbled, along with forty other mumbles from all around me.

"*Thank* you, Miss Gray! *Thank* you, Miss Gray!" someone squealed sarcastically in my ear.

I turned round to find Feargal (hood in regulation "up" position once again) pushing past me through the surge of escapees, staring at me as if I was a particularly horrible nodule of fungus.

"Look at *me*, Miss Gray – *I've* written a journal!" he squealed again, pulling a face while the lads surrounding him snickered away at their Lordship's excellent jest (not).

"Ignore him," Kyra ordered me, as I felt myself jostled out of the doorway and into the hall. "He only wears his hood up so he can catch the few brain cells he's got when they trickle out of his ears!"

Good old Kyra. She said that last bit really loudly, specially so Feargal and Co could hear. Feargal O'Leary might be fearless, but so is Kyra Davies, and it's times like that when I remember why being her friend is a good thing.

"What losers!" Jen hissed, narrowing her beady little eyes at the retreating, cackling bunch of be-hooded boys. "Anyway, see you two after lunch?"

"Yeah – if we can stand the excitement!" Kyra yawned, as we waved Jen off to the school canteen.

"Well," I muttered, heading towards the main exit with Kyra, and idly thinking about the mounds of peanut-butter sandwiches I was going to comfort-eat my way through at home, "That was horrible. What's Feargal's problem? What have I ever done to him...?"